Tamara took  **e heard m**

Vince tensed, too.

"Right," she agreed, following him.

Because he'd rather have her within reach, he didn't protest. He closed the front door and stopped, somewhat shielding her from seeing what was there.

She moved closer, squinting, needing the beam of his flashlight to see. It put her very close, too close. Standing up straight and trying to regain her composure, she shifted so she could see the words written on a piece of paper tacked to her door.

YOU BUY YOU DIE.

This time it looked like the sign maker had been in a hurry. The warning was in pencil, and whoever had made the sign had been more than angry. In five or six spots, the point of the pencil had gone right through the paper. Not only that, but the lines were in bold, dark letters.

"Another warning," Tamara muttered.

"No," Vince said. "This time, it's a promise."

Books by Pamela Tracy

Love Inspired Suspense   Love Inspired

Pursuit of Justice   *Daddy for Keeps*
The Price of Redemption
Broken Lullaby
Fugitive Family
Clandestine Cover-Up

PAMELA TRACY

lives in Arizona with a newly acquired husband (*Yes, Pamela is somewhat a newlywed. You can be a newlywed for seven years. Next year, we'll be oldlyweds.*) and a pre-schooler (*Newlymom is almost as fun as newlywed!*). She was raised in Omaha, Nebraska, and started writing at age twelve (a very bad teen romance featuring David Cassidy from the Partridge Family). Later, she honed her writing skills while earning a B.A. in Journalism at Texas Tech University in Lubbock, Texas (*and wrote a very bad science fiction novel that didn't feature David Cassidy*).

Pamela Tracy

Clandestine Cover-Up

Steeple
Hill®

Published by Steeple Hill Books™

STEEPLE HILL BOOKS

Steeple
Hill®

Recycling programs
for this product may
not exist in your area.

ISBN-13: 978-0-373-44367-3

CLANDESTINE COVER-UP

www.SteepleHill.com

Printed in U.S.A.

A good name is more desirable than great riches;
to be esteemed is better than silver or gold.
—*Proverbs* 22:1

To Sandra Lagesse, a friend extraordinaire.
Thank you for the shoulder to lean on,
the hand to hold, and the ear that listens.

ONE

YOUR NOT WANTED HERE

The words were written in dripping bloodred paint on the front door of the building Tamara Jacoby had just signed the final sale papers on. She'd been the proud owner for only twenty minutes. Her lawyer's mind, still sharp, still observant, wanted to change the *your* to *you're*. Her single female mind, still somewhat wounded, wanted to run to the car, jump in, lock the door and drive as far away as possible.

Wait, she'd already done that. That was how she'd arrived here in Sherman, Nebraska—far, far away from Arizona.

"It's not blood," she assured herself.

And William Massey is in jail, for a long, long time.

Still, to make sure, she whipped out her cell phone, dialed the 602 area code and spoke with a guard she knew at Florence Penitentiary.

Yes, William Massey is still in jail.

Which left Tamara wondering who on earth was after her now.

YOUR NOT WANTED HERE

Her sister Lisa, who lived here, called Sherman a safe little town.

Yeah, real safe.

She finally managed to control her breathing. Next, she unclenched her fingers and looked around.

A police cruiser turned the corner. The officer behind the wheel didn't even look Tamara's way, and she didn't wave him down.

She'd had enough interaction with the police to last a lifetime. First, thanks to her profession—lawyer. Last, thanks to the case that drove her out of Arizona—victim.

I am not a victim, she told herself.

No, she didn't want her first interaction with law enforcement in her new home to be a "rescue me" appeal. She wanted it to be an "I'm a force to be reckoned with" landing.

She fully intended to go back to being the kind of lawyer she'd been before William Massey fixated on her—successful, controlling and confident.

Right now, she'd settle for confident.

Tamara felt a chill. She wanted to blame the May weather, but the sudden chill had nothing to do with the rain. She'd had the chills every day for the past six months. Thoughts of William Massey had that effect on her. They had started the day he'd gone from client to deranged stalker. They'd doubled the day he'd gone from stalker to attacker.

Tamara took a tiny step forward. She had to do something. She couldn't stand on the sidewalk all day. She had to face whatever was in front of her. *Had to.* Otherwise, she might never practice law again.

Threats were part of the job.

Tamara studied the warning again. Not only was the wrong spelling used, but the letters were long and in some places the paint was almost too faint to read, while in others, it globbed. The vandal was probably right-handed, based on the slant of the graffiti. Also, whoever wrote the words was most likely tall, Tamara's height.

She looked up and blinked against the Nebraska sun, suddenly aware that she was busy assessing evidence as if preparing for trial.

She definitely didn't want the attention that would come with reporting this crime. Nor did she have the time. Not if she planned to turn this neglected old building, a building that had started life as a farmhouse and had last been used as a church, into a law office and get back on the fast track.

Did Sherman, Nebraska, even have a fast track?

Tamara pushed open the church's door, careful to avoid the paint, and took a step inside.

She suddenly stopped.

She'd seen dead animals before; they didn't scare her. But something about how the tiny mouse was laid out on the floor in front of her let her know the creature hadn't died a natural death.

It had died to prove a point.

YOUR NOT WANTED HERE.

She turned, tried to leave, and ran into something hard and unyielding.

She let out a squeal.

"Hey" came a deep voice. "I didn't mean to scare you."

Whoever blocked her way was all male. The scent of sweat combined with aftershave and heat permeated the room or at least the space directly around her. Her hand went inside her purse. Mace was at the ready, but warm, strong fingers clamped down hard on her elbow before she could snag the small tube and take aim.

"I'm not going to hurt you, Tamara," a calm voice stated. "It's Vince Frenci. I just got off work and was driving by and saw you standing on the sidewalk. You weren't moving, so I doubled back to see if everything was all right. What's going on?"

Her hand still clutched the mace. Tamara could feel her heart pounding, but she didn't want him to know he'd scared her. Some men fed off fear.

"There's a dead mouse," she managed to say. Her heart still beat a little too quickly. Her feet still refused to move.

You know Vince, she reminded herself. More than a year ago, they'd walked down the aisle together, thanks to her little sister's wedding. He'd been a little rough around the edges, but he was her brother-in-law's best friend. Which meant he probably knew her story, about the stalker and why she'd fled Phoenix, and why two weeks ago, she'd started the move to Sherman.

It's a safe little town.

He let go of her elbow and stepped back. Both of his hands went into the air as if he thought she'd shoot him.

She looked up at him and loosened her grip on the mace.

His hands left the air. "Look, if you're thinking about spraying me, don't bother. I'll just back out of here real quick like."

She finally let go of the mace. "I'm all right, and I remember you, Vince."

It would be hard to forget someone who looked like Vince Frenci. The man in front of her was working class through and through, with dark stubble, black spiky hair and piercing mahogany eyes. His clothes—blue

chambray shirt, tight jeans, oversize brown boots—
were worn for comfort and use, not for show.

"So, you want to tell me what's going on?" he asked.

"Can I blame the dead mouse for the warning on the
door?" she replied.

"You want to tell me what's really going on?"
Vince asked.

She shook her head.

"Well, you need to tell me something. Eventually, I'll
be the one to get rid of the paint on the door. I'll—"

"What do you mean, you'll be the one?"

"I've been the yardman for this property for more
than a decade. Every other Saturday, I mow, repair and
clean. If something's amiss here, I report it."

"Billy didn't tell me you worked for Lydia."

"Billy Griffin? How do you know him?" Vince asked.

Tamara held up the key. "I purchased this property
from him. Signed the purchase papers about an hour ago."

"Hmm," Vince said. "I didn't even know this place
was for sale. I wonder what Lydia's gonna think about
Billy selling off her property."

"She'll be grateful that her son cared enough to make
sure she was taken care of in a top-notch nursing home."

Vince shook his head. "I don't think so. If Lydia had
wanted this place sold, she'd have done it years ago."

"Why didn't she? I mean, what a waste of a com-
modity."

Vince shrugged. "If I had to guess, I'd say this plot
of land meant something to her family, but she never
said anything about fixing it up. She never let anyone
inside, not that I know of. I'm surprised Billy sold it,
but since he never really lived here in Sherman, maybe
he doesn't know the history of this place."

"Or maybe he doesn't care."

"If I know Lydia Griffin, she's gonna care and Billy will be getting an earful after she walks out of that nursing home on her own two feet."

Tamara had met Lydia Griffin last year. At that time, Lydia had been Tamara's niece's babysitter as well as Lisa's more than feisty landlord. Lydia had taken a fall two months ago, hit her head and broken her hip. The day she was supposed to get out of the hospital, she fell and broke her hip again. Now, she was slowly recuperating.

"I've been doing the yardwork since I was eighteen," Vince said. "That's one of the reasons I noticed you trespassing." Then, his expression changed from serious to teasing. "That and your red hair."

"I'm not trespassing," she reminded him. "I bought the place. It was only on the market for two weeks. Billy went looking for a quick sale. It was perfect timing for both of us."

"Makes sense," Vince said. "So," he asked, "you want to tell me about the door?"

"I'm actually more concerned about the mouse," she said. "Killing it and laying it out where I would see it the moment I stepped in the front door took more time and thought than writing on the door."

Funny, with him standing next to her the little mouse didn't look so menacing. She cleared her throat, trying to hold back the fear that was starting again. Sometimes Massey's memory was an almost tangible thing, letting her know that his clandestine and uninvited visit to her bedroom and its consequences may have happened six months ago, but still felt like yesterday.

Vince was looking at her as if she might break. She didn't want that.

Before he could ask another question, she asked, "When you did the yardwork, did you ever see anything unusual?"

"Like?"

"Like paint on the door."

"Most I've had to do is paint over graffiti on the outside walls. A while back someone was into gang signs, but there hasn't been any graffiti in the past year. Any chance your stalker followed you?"

"I just called the penitentiary that Massey's at. He hasn't been released."

"Could he have sent a friend?"

"I don't think he has any friends, but maybe he made one in jail," Tamara said. "I'll make a few calls later, find out if his cellmate or someone he palled around with has been paroled lately."

"You going to call the police?"

Tamara shook her head. For a moment, she wondered if Vince would call them. He seemed to be sizing her up. His expression didn't change so she couldn't tell if he thought she was incredibly brave for not alerting the authorities or undeniably stupid.

Tamara would have thought a client who didn't call the police was stupid.

One thing for sure, she was a better lawyer now because she empathized with her clients. Or she would, once she began practicing law again and had clients.

Vince stepped past her and entered the church. He glanced around. "Nothing else looks touched."

Considering the broken furniture and trash, his statement was almost comical, but Tamara knew from the walk-through of the building she and Billy had taken just a few days ago that broken furniture and debris were the only occupants of the no longer used church.

In a way, the old church was like Tamara, only she housed a broken dream, a broken relationship and broken spirit.

And if she could envision the old church as new and whole, then surely she could envision herself the same way.

Vince's whole life, he'd been turning around and cleaning up messes. Usually, his messes didn't look quite this good. Or this spooked. Taking that into consideration, Vince looked around for both a piece of cardboard and a section of newspaper.

Normally, it would have taken him just a second to dispose of the mouse. Instead, keeping in mind that Tamara watched his every move, he gently nudged the critter onto the cardboard, covered it with the newspaper and then took it outside.

When Vince finally returned, after fetching a flashlight from his truck, he studied her. She stood, looking pale, by the side of the front door. She chewed her bottom lip.

He hadn't noticed that habit when they'd walked down the aisle together at her sister's wedding. Maybe the nervous habit was new. Based on what she'd gone through the past six months, he could certainly understand. "You want me to take you home or do you want to walk around and make sure everything's where it should be?"

"I want to walk around."

Vince turned on the flashlight. It was dark enough

inside for the light to make a difference. "This grand old dame has plenty of life in her yet. I'm glad someone's finally going to do something with her. You know, I've never been inside. I always did the outside yardwork while Lydia worked on the inside."

"This is only my second time seeing the inside. Billy brought me over once, but he needed to catch a plane back to Denver for some family thing, so we didn't see much."

"I'm surprised a lawyer wouldn't demand a closer inspection."

"Oh," Tamara said, "I know a bargain when I see one. I can recognize potential, too. Plus, I trust the home inspector."

"This is probably the oldest building left on Main Street. The bookstore next door is old, but nothing like this." Vince stood in the middle of the room. A decade of dust shimmered in the air. Windows, curtainless, were so murky the outdoor sun couldn't find a spot to peek in.

Tamara walked into the center of the room. Her face softened a bit as she looked around. Some of the spooked look went away as she studied her purchase.

The church's meeting room housed roughly fourteen pews. Seven on each side. Some were broken; the others looked fine except for dust. A table was at the front of the room and a pulpit was right behind it. Both could use a good cleaning, but other than that, everything looked in fine shape.

"As soon as I can, I'm setting up practice. This will be my secretary's office. I'll have a couch as well as tables here. I'll add bookcases. I'll have a table set up with coffee and the daily newspaper. I'll put pictures on the wall showing pleased clients."

"This room's big enough," he agreed. "You could

almost retexture and build the bookcases right into the walls."

Knowing he might regret what he was about to do, Vince reached into his back pocket and took out his wallet. Then, he withdrew a business card and handed it to her.

She looked at his uniform with Konrad Construction embroidered on his left pocket. Then she looked again at the card. "You work on the side as a handyman and a lawn man?" she asked after looking the card over.

"I started at age ten mowing lawns. Lydia hired me when I was about thirteen. She had me do more than yards. She had me fixing fences and building sheds. We even redid the sidewalk in front of her house one year. I think she's to blame for my career choice. She's definitely to blame for my side job."

"I'll take this into consideration," Tamara said, sliding his card into her purse. Stepping over what looked to be a leg from one of the pews, she headed for a door to the right of the front table. It led to an empty room.

"What could this room have been?" she asked.

"It's probably where the church shared their meals. Maybe it doubled as a classroom."

She raised an eyebrow. "You attend church?"

"No, but I've helped build one. I do know that potlucks are a given and that there's never enough classroom space."

As they walked from room to room, he talked about replacing outdated fixtures and the cost of building materials. And with every word, he saw her relaxing a bit.

Maybe by the time they finished the walk-through she'd be willing to call the police.

They found two classrooms. Small chairs were stacked in corners. Chalkboards, warped beyond repair, hung on the walls. Next were two bathrooms. In black paint, someone had printed MEN on one. The smaller bathroom read WOMEN. He opened both doors, but didn't step in or invite her to look; instead he muttered something about copper pipe and enough space.

She'd wandered away from him around that time. He backed out of the restroom and saw that she was gone. He felt a moment of concern, and then he saw an open door and her footprints in the dust on the stairs.

She'd found the attic.

"This will be my office. This makes the whole venture worthwhile," she said, looking out the window at Main Street below. She left the window and her steps creaked in the silence.

"Old houses always make noise," she said. He could see she needed to believe it, needed to forget what was still written in graffiti on the front door.

"Yes," he agreed.

"Look at this desk! It's huge, it's mahogany, it's perfect." She looked around the room again. "Everything else in the room will have to go. First, those boxes stacked against the wall. Then, what's that old machine the size of a dishwasher?"

"That's an old copy machine. I saw one when we took down the old theater. Look at the crank handle. They probably used it to make their bulletins."

"Amazing," Tamara muttered. She wasn't talking about the copy machine. Right now she was looking at a single room full of dust, junk and old furniture. The look in her eyes said she wasn't seeing any of that, but what the room would look like after she finished with it.

She took one step toward the machine and froze as she heard movement downstairs. Vince tensed, too.

Critters weren't that loud, and people generally knocked when they entered.

Unless, of course, they were the kind of people who would paint a warning sign on a front door or leave a dead mouse.

"Wait here," he ordered.

Instead she followed him. Because he'd rather have her within reach, he didn't protest.

Slowly, they went through the building, listening for more noises, slowing when they heard one. As he led her out the front door, he tried not to remember the mouse or wonder who put it there and why.

He closed the front door and stopped, somewhat shielding her from seeing the words written on a piece of paper tacked to the door.

"What are you doing?" she asked, moving closer to see.

YOU BUY YOU DIE.

This time it looked like the sign maker had been in a hurry. The warning was in pencil and whoever had made the sign had been more than angry. In five or six spots, the point of the pencil had gone right through the paper. Not only that, but the words were in bold, dark letters.

"Another warning," Tamara muttered.

"No," Vince said. "This time, it's a promise."

TWO

Friday night, according to the police dispatcher, was not the best night for nonemergency responses. If Tamara wanted, she could wait a couple of hours for a squad car to show up. Or she could come down to the station and wait for an hour. Or she could wait until tomorrow.

Vince wanted to yank the phone out of her hand and fill the dispatcher in on Tamara's history with a stalker, especially since it didn't seem that she had any intention of doing so.

"I'll arrange to meet with an officer tomorrow," Tamara said.

As Tamara deposited her cell phone back into her purse, Vince asked, "So, you don't think it's important enough to tell them about the stalker?"

For a moment, he thought she'd clam up or tell him it was none of his business.

"There are three possibilities," she finally said. "One, these warnings weren't meant for me. That's my hope. Of course, more realistically, I may need to accept that my past has followed me and William Massey has an accomplice. Or, finally and even worse, I have something new to worry about."

That was what he'd been thinking. He didn't know whether to be relieved that she wasn't in denial about the threats or to be worried that she wasn't a screaming lunatic about the threats. He started to make a suggestion, but suddenly she was looking at him with the strangest expression.

"You know, it may not be a stalker. I mean Massey's notes were always of the 'I'm going to get you' variety. They always had an undertone that I belonged to him. Both the graffiti on the door and now this note seem to just want me to disappear."

He wanted to say that every stalker was different, but what did he know? "You want me to follow you to your sister's house?"

She raised an eyebrow. "Why would you follow me there?"

"It's where you're staying, right?"

"No, Lisa's nine months' pregnant. She's only been married a year and is busy building a home for a new husband and stepdaughter. There's a big difference between me coming for a short visit and me moving in. Trust me, she doesn't need another roommate."

"Okay, so where are you staying?" Vince asked.

"Billy's letting me rent his mother's upstairs apartment. It's the same one Lisa lived in before she married Alex. I just moved in this morning."

"Maybe you should call Alex? He'd come over."

Tamara shook her head. "Lisa doesn't need to be alone, and this is not their problem."

It wasn't his problem either, but as he followed her off the steps of the porch and then to her car, he couldn't shake the feeling that somehow her problem was about to become his problem.

"I'll follow you home," he said, opening her car door.

"I'd appreciate that."

It was well after ten when he finally parked his car behind Tamara's, and the nighttime sky offered little in the way of light. The streetlights, however, beamed a halfhearted welcome. Lydia's was the biggest house on the street. It also had the most character. It had, at one time, been his home away from home. A place he could go if things got a little difficult at home.

Stepping out of his truck, he walked leisurely over to Tamara's little red Jaguar. The sound of country music carried on the wind. She turned the car off before gathering up some papers and her purse plus a couple of shopping bags. He took the bags from her, half expecting her to protest, but maybe both the warnings and the mouse had subdued her.

He followed her to the bottom of an outdoor staircase. When Lydia had moved into the brick house, she had converted the upstairs to an apartment complete with its own entrance. Vince's mother said Lydia not only knew how to manage her money but how to create ways to make money.

Vince's mother was too busy trying to manage her sons to manage her money. When Vince was ten, his father had abandoned the family. That same year Vince's older brothers had moved out. For the next two years, Vince and his mother had moved from one apartment to another. They hadn't had much money. During that time, his mother had remarried, had Vince's little brother Jimmy, and got divorced. Vince became the man of the family.

When they got to the top of the stairs, Tamara unlocked the door, disappeared inside for a moment and then returned to relieve him of the bags.

"Thanks," she murmured softly. "I was getting a little spooked back there at the church. You made some pretty bad moments not so horrible. I do appreciate your help." Then she smiled and closed the door.

Leaving him outside, feeling as if he'd just missed an opportunity he hadn't even realized was offered. That realization was followed by the certainty that his initial attraction to her flowing red hair was really nothing.

Nope, it was her smile that did him in.

For the first time in months, Tamara fell into bed without going through a paranoid routine of checking her front door's lock and all the windows about a dozen times.

Tonight when she crawled into bed, her last thought was *I'm tired.* She didn't make it to *I wish I could fall asleep.* Instead, she fell asleep.

For two whole minutes.

And then, her eyes went to the clock by her bedside. Midnight.

It had all started at midnight. William Massey's first phone call. Tamara burrowed under the blankets and, even though her clock didn't make any noise, she covered her ears.

She almost wished she could blame Massey, but tonight what kept her from sleeping was the sudden realization that most likely Massey wasn't involved with the threatening warnings she had received.

No, he struck at midnight.

On Saturday morning, Vince drove to Tamara's apartment to check on her.

Her car was gone. There was no cause for worry, he

thought. He headed for the church. But her car wasn't there either. Okay, a slight cause for worry. He checked the only other place he could think of—her sister's house. She wasn't there. Finally, he spotted her car. It was the first time he'd ever felt relief at finding who he was looking for at the police station.

Checking his watch, he grimaced. Today was pretty much mapped out thanks to a promise he made his mother to help his great-uncle Drew. He turned his truck toward what used to be the outskirts of town.

Vince pulled into the dirt driveway leading up to his uncle's trailer. Drew opened the front door once Vince started taking things out of the bed of his truck. Slowly, Drew stepped down onto his front step, glared and spit on the ground. "What are you doing, boy?"

In his younger days, according to those who remembered, Drew had been over two hundred pounds, six foot two and a contender with attitude. Now, past eighty, Drew was a walking advertisement for skin and bones and bad attitude.

Drew knew exactly why Vince had shown up this morning.

Vince answered anyway. "I'm cleaning up your yard. You only have thirty days, remember, before you start getting hefty fines."

Drew clutched at the screen door. It kept him steady. "I'll shoot anyone who comes on my land in thirty days."

Sad thing was, Vince almost believed the old man. "Uncle Drew, just let me take care of this and then you won't need to worry."

Like his uncle had once been, Vince was over six foot, weighed just over two hundred pounds and had attitude. The difference was, Vince had learned to control his attitude. Not that a good attitude was helping to deal with Drew today.

Even with his missing weight, stooped height and outward frailty, Drew's voice still had a guttural edge. "Ain't worried. Don't need any help. Git."

"I'm not *gitting*." Vince didn't move, and Drew stomped into the trailer—no doubt heading to the phone to call Vince's mother. He wouldn't get far there. She was terrified at the thought of Drew winding up home-less and showing up on her doorstep.

Mom still had Jimmy at home, and right now Jimmy was at what his mother called an awkward stage. He still needed approval but insisted he could make his own decisions. From what Mom said, most of Jimmy's deci-sions right now were wrong.

Vince wasn't too worried. He'd survived puberty.

Come to think of it, maybe Vince should have a talk with Jimmy.

If nothing else, getting Jimmy out here to help pull weeds might be an opportunity that benefited both of them. Vince could pay Jimmy, and Jimmy could start saving for the car he wanted. One brief phone call later, Vince knew that idea was a bust.

Even at age sixteen, Jimmy was terrified of Uncle Drew.

Vince started pulling the weeds growing past his knees in the front yard. Every twenty minutes or so, as perfectly timed as a cuckoo on a clock, Drew would open the screen door, curse and spit and then retreat.

Things got even more interesting a few hours later when Miles Pynchon, minister of the Main Street Church, pulled up in a fairly new pickup and shouted, "Need some help?"

"I've got a handle on this," Vince said. "You might not want your sons to hear what my uncle Drew has to say."

"They've heard your uncle Drew many a time," Miles said. "We live just over the fence. Drew's inspired a sermon or two. Anytime you want to attend services and come listen, you're invited. Now, the boys and I have about three hours to spare. Tell us where to start."

"So far, I've been working with two guidelines. If it's trash, throw it away. If it's too heavy to move, leave it alone."

"All of it looks like trash," one boy muttered.

It only took five minutes for Drew to notice his visitors. Funny, Vince had grown up in a world where cursing was the rule not the exception. Never had he noticed just how *bad* it sounded, at least in front of kids. It made him wish more than ever that Miles and his sons would leave and let Vince work in peace.

Instead, Miles sang while he loaded old pieces of wood, broken buckets, all kinds of signs, cans of paint and smelly tarps into the back of Vince's truck. He started with tunes from the Beatles, switched to James Taylor and, by the time the sun started to descend, he'd worked his way to gospel songs. Some Vince knew; others he did not.

In between songs Miles invited Drew and Vince to attend church on Sunday. Drew had two words for the invitation; the second word was *no*. Vince also shook his head. His mother had gone to church a time or two. She'd never felt welcome. He doubted he'd feel much different.

"I can even offer Drew a ride," Miles offered.

The teenage boys gave each other the guarded look that all teenagers share when it comes to the actions of their parents. Vince couldn't help it. He laughed.

"We all appreciate you cleaning up his yard," Miles said. "He scares most of the neighbors. Some complain just because they hope it will somehow cause him to move."

"That's not going to happen. The more people complain, the more he'll dig his feet in," Vince commented.

Miles nodded. "What happened to your uncle, Vince, to make him like this? Such an empty life."

"My mom says he's always been like this. My father blamed Drew's time in the military. Drew spent time in Alaska and then Vietnam, but he was over in Vietnam in the early sixties before anything really happened." Vince thought about it for a moment. "Except maybe drugs."

They worked silently for a moment. Then Vince asked, "Hey, Miles, do you know Tamara Jacoby?"

"I've met her a few times. Why?"

Vince waited a moment, hoping the minister would say more. When he didn't, Vince continued, "Did Alex and Lisa fill you in on what happened back in Phoenix with Tamara?"

Miles stopped working. "They did."

Vince checked to make sure the boys couldn't hear. "She bought the old Amhurst Church. I stopped by there last night when I saw her standing on the sidewalk. Someone had painted 'you're not wanted here' on the door. Then, she found a dead mouse inside."

"Think it's Massey?"

That the preacher remembered the stalker's name told Vince how much the family had confided in their minister.

"She called someone she knows who told her that Massey's still in prison. It gets worse. While she and I were both inside, someone left a threatening note on the door."

"You tell Alex?"

"No. It didn't seem my place. I was there when she called the police. This morning she went by the police station and filed a report."

"That young lady's been through enough," Miles said.

"Can you talk to her?" Vince asked. "Maybe get her to stay with Lisa and Alex for a while."

"I'll try. She's only been to church once since she's been here. I started to welcome her, but she ducked away. Maybe you could bring her?"

"Nice try," Vince declined.

The door to the trailer opened. Drew hobbled out and crawled into his old truck, muttering, "Miserable excuses for human beings," before driving toward town.

"Must be grocery day," Vince said.

"No," Miles answered. "Grocery day is Monday. He'd never go to the grocery store on a Saturday, too crowded."

They watched the ancient Ford truck disappear from sight.

For the past half hour, Miles sang a few more gospel songs. His voice was low, and the songs were poignant. They fit the mood. Vince had no doubt the minister would talk to Tamara, offer assistance and even maybe counsel. Problem was, Miles Pynchon was in charge of a whole congregation. Vince wasn't sure of the number, but based by the size of the church building, Vince figured more than two hundred members. There was only so much time Miles could give to Tamara, especially if she wasn't asking for help.

At just after five o'clock, the Pynchon boys followed their dad to his truck. They took enough parts to make either a lawn mower that ran like a motorcycle or a motorcycle that also functioned as a lawn mower. Either

way, the boys looked intrigued. The minister took home
a wooden cross, splintered in places, and a Bible so old
its leather binding was all but in shreds.

One man's junk was another man's treasure.

As Vince headed for his truck, he took one last look
at his uncle's property. Thanks to his efforts and that of
the Pynchons, the yard had a few clear areas and even
something of a path. Not that Drew needed a path. Vince
doubted the old man cared to walk in his backyard or
even knew what all was in it.

Drew's backyard was quite a bit like Drew's life—
filled with a lot of junk that no one really cared about.

Vince paused.

His own backyard consisted of sheds and tools and
toys. Things that right now, during his prime, seemed
important. It all could count as clutter; it could all eventually turn to junk.

Funny how thinking about Uncle Drew and then
thinking about Tamara really made a man think about
what should be important.

THREE

As Vince drove the streets of Sherman, he pondered just exactly what he was doing.

Adding one more worry to his life, he realized.

Worrying about and taking care of his family had been a full-time job since he was ten.

He didn't want to feel responsible for even one more person.

Which, he told himself, was why he shouldn't be thinking about Tamara Jacoby. Thing was, he couldn't seem to stop.

All because she was a redhead with haunted green eyes, a quick tongue and a killer smile.

He parked in front of her house and knocked on her door a few moments later, trying to think of just what he'd say.

He'd never been at a loss for words with a female. He was the prankster, the stud, the man of the moment. Everyone's friend, no one's confidant. He'd never thought about what to say to a woman because he'd never had to. He'd never really cared much one way or the other. If he started thinking about a woman too much, he stopped—stopped thinking, stopped calling, stopped taking them out. He didn't want to let any woman too close. He already had too many responsibilities to his family.

No one answered his knock.

He hurried down the stairs, trying to tell himself he was glad she wasn't home. His steps slowed when he got to her car.

It didn't matter how tired he was. Unless he found out she was okay, he wasn't going to get any rest tonight. He took out his cell phone and called her brother-in-law, Alex. No answer. So, he tried Alex's wife, Lisa. Surely, if anyone knew what Tamara was up to, it would be her sister.

As Lisa's cell phone rang he tried to think of the best scenario. Maybe the reason Alex hadn't answered and now Lisa wasn't answering was because Lisa had gone into labor. Of course if that was true, maybe Tamara had run from the apartment, zoomed right past her own car, and made decent time—on foot—to the hospital.

Scenario two, she was actually inside the apartment sound asleep and hadn't heard his knock.

He liked both ideas. They were so much better than the other options his imagination could supply.

"Hey, Vince, sorry it took me so long to answer. I didn't hear the phone buzzing in my purse. What's up?" Lisa didn't sound stressed enough to be in labor. And in the background, he could hear the muted sounds of a softball game in progress. He looked across the street at the shimmering lights of a ballpark.

"Do you know where Tamara is?"

"Sure, she's here with us. Alex's church team is playing tonight."

"I'll be right there." It made perfect sense, Vince thought. She'd not need to drive the car across the street to the park. It was just as quick to walk. Which was what he started to do. His steps quickened the closer he got because he didn't see two redheads, just one.

Lisa Cooke, Tamara's sister, nine months' pregnant, and who should be taking it easy, was in the stands cheering on her husband.

"Hey!" Lisa called. She nudged her stepdaughter, Amy, whose nose was in a book, and they both scooted over, giving him some room to sit down. "So, you want to tell me what's up with you and my sister?" she asked.

"Where is she?"

"She didn't want to use her cell phone and watch the game at the same time. She's been slumming behind the snack bar for the past half hour."

"Can you see her?"

Lisa pointed. "The preacher already wants her for third base. He says if she shows that much passion for a phone call, just think what she'd muster for a play-off game."

"Who's she talking to?" Vince asked.

"I'm pretty sure she's still on the phone with Terry, which amazes me since I thought they weren't talking."

"Terry?"

"Her ex-fiancé."

Vince started to stand, then thought better of it. He patted Amy on the head. She giggled and went back to reading.

The bleachers weren't built with big men in mind. Vince found a place to stretch his feet and managed to knock over Lisa's purse. After he righted it, he asked, "Did you know she bought the old Amhurst Church building?"

"Yes, and I think it's great."

"If you think it's great, then she didn't tell you

about yesterday. Someone had painted a warning on the front door."

Lisa glanced at her daughter, who wasn't paying the slightest attention, and asked, "What did it say?"

"You're not wanted here."

Lisa's lips tightened. "She didn't say a word. She thinks just because I'm pregnant I'm made of glass. Did she say anything about William Massey? You think that's why she's talking to Terry?"

"She called someone yesterday. I'm not sure it was this Terry guy or not. Seems Massey's still in jail."

"Could he have—"

"Tamara said she'd find out. That's basically why I'm here. I was with her at the church building last night. I even saw her safe into her apartment. Today, I can't seem to get her out of my mind. I can't believe she didn't tell you any of this."

"She didn't tell me because I'd have insisted she come stay with us. She probably thinks she'd be in the way or somehow put us in danger."

"I don't think she should be in her apartment alone," Vince said. "Not until the authorities find out who is leaving threatening messages."

"Messages," Lisa said. "You mean there was more than one?"

Before he could answer, the people around them screamed and jumped up. It didn't take long to figure out the game had ended with Alex hitting a triple and bringing two runners in.

The remaining fans started gathering their kids and belongings. It didn't look like tonight would be one of those lingering, "let's go out for pizza" kind of nights. Glancing at his watch, Vince realized it was late even for a Saturday game. It was well past nine, it was dark, and there was church in the morning for most people there.

Lisa didn't smile as she made sure Amy had everything and then carefully climbed down from one stair to the next. When they reached the bottom, Tamara stood waiting. The look on her face clearly showed her displeasure.

"Vince, when did you get here?" Tamara asked.

"A good half hour ago."

"Long enough to tell me what you didn't bother to tell me," Lisa said.

"It might be nothing," Tamara insisted. "Massey never sent me a 'get lost' message. It was always a 'you're mine' kind of message. Besides, I've called the victim information and notification hotline three times, and they say Massey hasn't been released. Terry says that Massey hasn't left jail. He hasn't had any visitors, either. And, apparently, his cellmate is a white-collar criminal who only wants to do his time and get out. Massey's not a threat."

"Someone's a threat," Vince reminded her.

Tamara nodded. "Only thing new in Massey's life is some hotshot lawyer he's hired. Terry says the guy's trying to get some of my testimony stricken because of lawyer/client confidentiality."

"Can they do that?" Lisa asked.

"Since I met Massey while I was assisting the attorney who was representing him on a separate matter, yes. Never mind that, after he started stalking me, my firm severed representation. His attorney is going to claim that while testifying, I had knowledge that I wouldn't have had if I had not been present during the first case. He's going to go over every transcript of my testimony and look for key phrases, similarities, any time I might have used legal jargon instead of acting like a witness."

"It doesn't seem right," Vince said.

"It's exactly what I'd be doing if I were his new lawyer. They're scrounging for reasonable doubt," Tamara said. "So, now, along with trying to figure out who painted the words on my door, I need to worry about the possibility of Massey's release."

"Vince." Alex, out of breath, and still flying high from being instrumental in the winning run, chose that moment to join them. Grinning, he reached out to shake Vince's hand. "Good to see you." Alex let go of Vince's hand and reached for his wife.

She didn't move toward him. Instead, through gritted teeth, she muttered, "We're going to have a little talk with my big sister."

Concern flickered across Alex's face.

"No, not about me," Lisa quickly assured him.

He looked from Lisa, to Vince, to Tamara. His daughter was the only other one present who didn't have a clue what was going on.

"Great hit, Dad," Amy said, giving him a hug. She was soon skipping toward the parking lot with another little girl about the same age.

"Okay, what's going on?" Alex asked.

"Tamara's not safe," Lisa said quickly. "She needs to move in with us for a while."

"I'm not sure if I'm safe or not," Tamara insisted. "But if I'm not safe, you guys are the last ones I'm going to endanger." She looked pointedly at Lisa's stomach. "In a few days, you'll have another baseball player to worry about, and I'm certainly not going to let my problems become your problems."

Alex turned to Vince. "Tell me everything."

It took all of ten minutes, and Tamara only interrupted once a minute.

When they finished, Alex simply shook his head, dropped his bat bag to the ground and went back to the dugout. When Vince saw what Alex had in mind, he followed.

Behind him, he could hear Tamara's protest and then Lisa's voice beginning to rise. Tamara immediately hushed.

Jake Ramsey, Sherman's sheriff, already had his softball gear packed and was ready to head toward his vehicle. He looked happy to see Alex—no doubt, anyone who could hit a triple during overtime had the sheriff's approval—but he didn't look as happy to see Vince.

No surprise there.

Vince and the sheriff were well acquainted thanks to the run-ins with the law of Vince's uncle, dad and brothers. Okay, Vince hadn't been completely immune to getting into trouble. He just happened to be the Frenci who learned from his mistakes.

"Tell the sheriff everything," Alex ordered.

"I think the sheriff already knows everything," Vince said. "Tamara was at the police station this morning. But that doesn't mean he's doing everything he can."

"What do you think I should be doing, Vince?" Jake asked.

"More."

"You're right," Jake said. "There is more I should be doing. Questioning you, for one. You arrived at the scene rather conveniently."

"I got off work at five. The church is right on my way home. Plus, you know I work there."

"What made you stop this time?" Jake asked.

"I saw Tamara just standing there, not moving. It wasn't that hard to tell something was wrong."

"Never took you for being a concerned citizen."

Jake was cop through and through. His grandfather had been sheriff, then his father and now Jake. Vince's family helped keep Jake's family in business. Drew had been in and out of jail his whole life. Vince's father, pretty much the same until he disappeared. Vince's brothers, especially his next oldest brother, Mickey, knew the facility well.

Vince had already been behind bars once. When he was sixteen, he'd been caught stealing a car. His brother Darren had actually stolen the car, but Vince was driving it when the police cruiser had pulled up behind them.

Jake's father had been the sheriff back then.

"Because of Alex, here, I knew some of what Tamara had been going through back in Phoenix. There's not a chance I'd just drive by if she needed help."

"And I'm glad you stopped, but I'm not glad you're dragging everybody into my business," Tamara said, walking over to stand next to Vince.

"Forewarned is forearmed," Vince started.

Alex finished for him. "This is our business, too, and—"

"And I would have informed you about what's going on once I figured out exactly what *is* going on," Tamara remarked.

"It could be a month before that happens," Vince said snidely. "Sheriff Ramsey, with all due respect, you need…"

Tamara put her finger to her lips, and Vince hushed.

"I can tell you what the sheriff's doing," Tamara said.

"He's assigned deputies to drive by my apartment every hour. He's waiting for a call back from the detective in Phoenix who handled my case. He's advised me to move in with Lisa and Alex. I'm the one who wanted to hold off for a while. If there's something that can be done, he's been doing it."

Jake looked at Vince. "For years, you've been taking care of the grounds at that old church. I'd think you'd know if something funny was happening around the place."

"Nothing funny has happened except for Tamara buying it and nobody, including me, realizing it was for sale."

Before Jake could reply, he got a call and took off at a jog toward his car. Vince followed Alex and Tamara back to the bleachers. Lisa tapped her foot impatiently.

"Well, did you find out anything?" Lisa asked.

"Just that there's nothing yet to find out," Tamara joked.

It was a feeble attempt, and Vince admired her all the more for making the effort.

"Spend the night at our place," Lisa said. "If you don't, I won't get a wink of sleep."

"The sheriff has a deputy driving by every hour," Tamara told Lisa. "I've got about ten phone calls to make and I'm expecting about ten phone calls back."

"Spend the night," Alex urged. "Tomorrow morning things will look better, and maybe Lisa won't be so stressed."

Tamara glanced at Lisa, and finally at Vince. "Okay, it's probably a good idea. Not that anything's happened today. Everything happened yesterday."

Alex, Lisa and Amy headed for their van while Vince walked Tamara across the parking lot. His truck was parked behind her car, and it would be easy to make sure she got what she needed from the apartment and then was on her way to Lisa's place.

As they walked, he half expected her to give him grief for telling her sister about the warnings, but she was quiet. A bit too quiet.

"Are you all right?" he said.

"No, not really. I haven't been all right since all this started. And I hate that it's starting again—the not knowing, the people offering to help when they haven't a clue how."

"That would be me."

"Yeah, in many ways, that would be you. It's just as bad watching people who you expect to be there for you pull away."

"That would be your ex-fiancé, Terry?"

She didn't answer. And, in typically lawyer fashion, her nonanswer was louder than words.

He didn't know how to respond. This wasn't the time for small talk or jokes. When she got to the edge of the sidewalk, she stopped.

"We can cross the street now," he said quietly after a moment. "There's no cars."

She didn't move, and suddenly he remembered her stance yesterday, when she stood on the old church's sidewalk, unmoving. She looked exactly the same.

He looked across the street at Lydia's house. It was too dark to see the door.

But it wasn't the door she was looking at. It was her car. The tires facing them were flat. Not just a bit low but full-out, no-longer-round flat.

"You didn't have any flat tires when I arrived," he growled. He took two steps into the street, thought again and turned around to take her by the hand. Together they circled her car.

All four tires were destroyed.

"This only proves," he pointed out, "that you need to be with family, friends, until we sort this out, because somebody's out to get you."

"No," she said. "Because whoever's out to get me is willing to get whomever I'm with."

All four of Vince's tires were destroyed, too.

FOUR

The next morning, Vince's brother took care of the tires. After Darren checked out the rest of the car, Tamara packed a suitcase and headed back to Phoenix. She'd been very lucky when she'd arrived in Sherman two weeks ago. She'd signed a lease on her sister's old apartment, already furnished, and then scouted the town for a place to hang her shingle. She'd lucked into the old church because her landlord was the one selling it. Now she hoped severing her ties in Phoenix would be as easy. She needed to deal with putting her condo on the market, packing up or putting into storage her belongings, which she'd left with middle sister Sheila, and trying to find out just exactly what Massey's new lawyer was up to.

It took two weeks for her to change the For Sale condo to a For Rent condo after realizing nothing was selling; two weeks to recognize that the belongings she'd left at her sister's really belonged at the Goodwill since she didn't really need anything; and two weeks to realize that while physically William Massey was behind bars, figuratively, he was still very much a presence.

During his trial, he'd acted as his own lawyer. All that did was confirm for authorities just how dangerous he was. A class-three felony and her testimony put him behind bars for two years.

And already he was filing an appeal that had potential. Thanks to a new lawyer who was all over the minute details of attorney-client privilege, two years might not happen.

The entire drive back to Sherman, she debated her next move.

Stay in Phoenix? Move to Sherman? Find a job in New York City? Surely she could get lost there?

In the end, Sherman won. She'd already started rebuilding her life, even purchased her own building. In truth, she wanted to be in Sherman. She wanted to be near her sister and soon-to-be-born nephew. She wanted a small-town practice. But more than anything she wanted to feel safe again.

If that was even possible after the warnings and dead mouse.

Sheriff Jake Ramsey had phoned her in Phoenix a half-dozen times over the past two weeks. He'd checked out her place of business and her place of residence more than once. He'd taken fingerprints, and questioned her neighbors. He figured the target of the threats was Vince, or more likely, one of Vince's brothers. If Tamara hadn't found the note, Vince would have found it, shrugged and tossed it. Just another day in the life of a Frenci.

Tamara knew better. Yes, Vince had a connection to the building and grounds, but she had a gut feeling that the warnings and the mouse weren't meant for him. After all, what were the odds that someone would go looking to slash his tires, find him at Tamara's apartment, and then think, *Oh, boy, let's slash her tires, too!*

As she pulled into the parking lot of the old church,

she reconsidered yet again. Maybe she should have thought a little harder, waited a little longer before making an offer on this particular building.

The roof looked sound although a rickety weather-vane leaned dangerously to the left. The small parking lot to the right of the building would need to be repaved. The walkway, too. The front porch would need to be both refitted and repainted. The front door looked sturdy enough if somewhat odd with the brown wrapping paper taped over the graffiti.

At least there was no new warning sign today.

She walked around the church. The lawn looked a little overgrown. It made sense. Since Tamara had purchased the church, Vince no longer worked for or was paid by Lydia. She needed to hire a handyman—and soon.

Reaching in her purse, she pulled out a business card.

The card said, "Vincent Frenci, handyman and general repair." She knew the phone number on the card by heart.

She was pretty sure he wasn't at church. At least, he hadn't been there the one Sunday she had visited with her sister.

She'd taken the card out at least three times a day, each time telling herself she wasn't going to call him when she got back to Sherman. No, she'd hire a land-scaping firm.

But she dialed his number anyway.

It was totally against her character.

Yet exactly what she'd been planning to do every day for the past two weeks.

Vince parked his truck, exited and made his way toward the porch. Tamara was sitting on the front stoop, leaning back, and looking all the world like she was comfortable. Sensibly, she'd shed her jacket, but she still looked too warm in a white button-down shirt tucked into blue creased slacks. Black heels completed the outfit.

Her eyes were closed. Vince would have given the keys to his beloved truck just to know what she was thinking, what had put the half smile on her face.

He doubted she relaxed often, especially since a stalker had made her his target.

He stopped and looked down at her, enjoying the view. "Well, Miss Jacoby, I hear you are still the proud owner of a church."

She opened her green eyes, not looking the least bit perturbed that he'd snuck up on her.

"I'm not so easily scared off," she said. "Nothing's happened for two weeks."

"You haven't been here for things to happen," he pointed out.

"William Massey is still in jail. The courts are looking over transcripts trying to determine if his rights were violated during the trial because of my testimony. But—" she looked over at Vince "—my ex-fiancé says there's nothing to worry about."

He settled down on the stoop next to her, noticing how much bigger he was than she. His legs stretched two steps farther than hers. His arms, well, he wasn't quite sure what to do with them so he simply leaned back, using them as anchors.

She didn't move over. He liked that.

"Are you worried?"

"Of course! I'm taking this very seriously. I, more than anyone, know how out of hand a situation can get. I'm watching my back. And—" she sobered "—I don't for a minute think any of this is aimed at you. Jake is way off."

"Jake *is* way off," Vince agreed. "I've gone back and forth a dozen times. I wish the warnings were aimed at me rather than you."

"So, why do you think your tires were slashed?" Tamara asked.

"I think my tires were slashed because someone is bothered by the fact I'm near you," Vince said simply.

"That's silly."

He didn't answer, just looked at her, until she nodded. "This means that anyone near me is in danger. Exactly what I worried about and why I don't want to stay with my sister and her husband right now. And maybe why I made a mistake coming back here. Yet, here I am. It's a crazy world."

"How crazy is it?" Vince asked. Maybe if he knew just what had happened, what the papers hadn't reported, and what Tamara had really gone through, then maybe what was happening now would make sense since it involved him. "Tell me about Massey."

Tamara blanched. For a moment, he thought she'd walk away and leave him sitting there. Finally, she softly asked, "How much do you know?"

"I know that your firm was representing him and that he took a liking to you. I know he sent you love letters and followed you. I know he broke into your apartment and you managed to fight him off."

She no longer looked relaxed. She looked rigid, uncomfortable, and Vince almost said, *Let's do this later,* but then she started talking.

"You know a lot," she acknowledged. "Working for a top law firm really helped keep the reporters at bay.

The media had to be careful with every word lest they let something slip that either put me in danger or compromised the case."

"You mean the papers didn't want to be sued by your firm."

"That, too," Tamara agreed. "Why should they be so different? Everybody, my neighbors, my coworkers, they all started being so careful around me. They talked the sympathy game, but I could tell, they were mostly grateful that what was happening to me wasn't happening to them. However, my sisters acted with righteous indignation. Lisa, right away, wanted me to come stay with her. Sheila wanted me to fight. Both didn't think the law acted fast enough. Terry, my fiancé, couldn't keep his annoyance at bay. See, my stalker interfered with other cases—both mine and his—and eventually Massey interfered with social events.

"I should have trusted my gut with Massey," Tamara said morosely. "The minute he showed up at our law firm, my skin crawled. He looked like such an ordinary guy, but it took only a minute for me to recognize that the look of detachment was fake and that he'd mastered the art of mind games. We sat in the firm's conference room and I wrote down everything he said. Now, I look back, and I realize I was such a different person back then."

"Why did he hire your firm in the first place?" Vince asked.

"He was accused of purposely running a mother and her daughter off the road."

"Reckless endangerment?"

"It was almost vehicular manslaughter but the woman pulled through so her lawyer was going for aggravated assault. She'd recently filed a restraining order against Massey. Seems he'd been following her and had even approached her a couple times asking her out. When she refused he did things like grab a grocery bag out of her hand and fling it to the ground. They had a witness for that. He'd show up at the daughter's school and pretend to be a relative sent to pick her up. The school called the police. By the time they got there, he was gone. But the girl's teacher identified him."

"Seems pretty cut-and-dried."

"Yeah, but the letter of the law has to do with intent. He rammed the mother's car but claimed his intent wasn't to harm. Plus, the mother was driving on a suspended license. She'd lost hers thanks to a DUI."

"Was she intoxicated when the accident happened?"

"No, but it was still something we would bring up in court, trying to get him either acquitted or get him a lesser sentence."

"So, what happened with that case? Did he start stalking you right away?"

"Yes, he started stalking me right away. First it was a thank-you card and an offer to dinner. Then, it was flowers every day to the office. We released him as a client. I got a restraining order. He changed tactics quickly. The notes stopped, the flowers stopped. He painted the words *You belong to me* on my door," Tamara said next.

"Red paint like here?"

"Red must be the color criminals like best."

"No wonder you were standing so still that first day. I thought at first I'd have to pick you up, like a piece of furniture, and carry you somewhere."

"He started calling every night at midnight and he'd play music. He had a favorite song. To this day I can't get the first verse out of my head. It's all about love and waiting until no one else is around."

"Hard to believe," Vince said.

"Massey broke into my condo the night Terry and I broke up. I was upset, and for the first time in months, I let my guard down. I was too busy crying to look over my shoulder."

"He followed you inside?"

"To this day, I don't know. I'd been home for maybe an hour. I went to bed, but I wasn't asleep. Then, he was there. When I hit him with the flashlight I'd been keeping by the bed, it sliced into his forehead. The blood gushed so quickly I had time to push him away from me and run from the apartment to my next-door neighbors. He left blood on my bedsheets. It was enough to seal his fate."

"Some people belong in jail. Which is where Massey is," Vince reminded her. "Somebody else is pulling our chains now. My gut feeling is that it's this building you need to stay away from. There has to be some reason why Lydia left it to rot. You should get rid of it and find somewhere else for your office."

She blinked, and he could see that the idea that the church was the catalyst hadn't occurred to her. Unfortunately, she wouldn't give up that easy, which meant he needed to stick around a while. Since she wasn't going to agree with his suggestion, he made another. "So, I take it instead of letting it rot, you're going to hire me on to help renovate."

"Why make some other handyman a target when you already fit the bill?"

He liked that, even with all that was going on, she still had a sharp tongue. Working with her and for her would never be dull.

FIVE

On Monday, after several hours of cleaning trash away from the church's main room, Tamara heard a noise. It sounded like a creak that accompanied a footfall. She silently straightened and slowly turned, wishing her back wasn't to the front door. Her purse, with the mace inside, was in the attic on top of the desk.

Did she have time to run and get it?

"Hello," a woman called loudly. Then seeing that Tamara was right in the main room, she grinned. "Oops, didn't see you there."

The woman at the door definitely didn't look dangerous. She looked friendly and welcoming.

"I'm Angela. I own the bookstore next door. I was wondering if you'd like to go across the street for lunch. Since we're about to be neighbors and fellow businesswomen, I thought we should maybe get to know each other."

"Thanks for the offer, but I'm covered with dust and look a mess."

"Oh, that doesn't make any difference. Tali and Sharon have been watching you all morning. They want to meet you, too. This is a great street. Most of the merchants work together. Sharon has my business cards on a table in her restaurant lobby. I send people over there to eat. Never thought this old church would ever stop being vacant. So, you're a lawyer? You don't look like a lawyer."

Tamara had to laugh. Usually, people didn't have any trouble believing her vocation. "I'm a lawyer. Right now I just happen to be a lawyer masquerading as a handyman. I'm opening up my own practice."

"Well, I admire any lawyer willing to get her hands dirty. Come have lunch. My treat."

"But I'm covered with—"

"It's after one, the lunch rush is over. There are probably only ten people at the restaurant."

There were twelve, but that was counting Tali and Sharon Rasmussen, who joined Angela and Tamara the moment they were seated.

Tali was a big, black man who didn't fit the persona of who Tamara imagined would be the owner of an Italian restaurant. He towered over his wife, who was short, curly haired and animated.

Actually, they both were animated and—Angela was right—they were both eager to meet her.

"We're glad somebody's doing something with the property," Tali said. "It's been neglected for so long."

"Not neglected," his wife said. "Lonely. Vincent keeps up the grounds and such, so it hasn't hurt property values, but talk about a waste of space."

"So what are you planning to do with the building?" Tali asked.

She started to answer, but before she could, he continued, "We've seen you with Vincent. Are you planning to hire him? We can recommend him. He works for Konrad Construction during the week. They remodeled our house."

"And Vincent hired on afterward and put up a shed for us," Sharon added.

Tali pooh-poohed, "That took all of an hour. I could have done it had you given me time."

"I gave you time," Sharon disagreed. "We had the building materials for over a year."

"Tell them what you're going to do with the old church," Angela interrupted.

"Open my own law practice," Tamara said easily.

Tali leaned back. "Ah…then, we heard right."

Before he could say anything else, the waitress came, orders were given, and Sharon took over the conversation before her husband could.

"We were saying that a lawyer is just what Vince needs."

"Sharon," Angela warned.

"What? You think Tamara isn't going to find out about—"

"I already know Vince," Tamara said. "He's best friends with my sister's husband."

Angela nodded. "That's why you looked familiar. I can't believe I didn't see the likeness earlier. I knew I'd seen the red hair before. You're Lisa's sister."

"Big sister." Tamara turned to Sharon and asked, "What about Vince needing a lawyer?"

"Not Vince," Sharon said. "His family. Mainly Vince's brothers and definitely his uncle Drew."

Tamara took a drink of her iced tea. "Vince hasn't mentioned them."

Of course Vince hadn't mentioned his family. A year ago, during the wedding, their focus had been on Lisa and Alex. Two weeks ago, when Vince came to Tamara's rescue, it had all been about Tamara. Yesterday, on the porch, it had been all about Tamara again.

"So," she encouraged, "Vince has an interesting family?"

They all nodded their heads.

"He has an active family," Tali said.

"Not like they used to be," Angela said. "Vince and Darren both are decent sorts. Vince built the bookcases for my store. Darren works on my car, and he doesn't charge an arm and a leg."

"How big is Vince's family?" Tamara asked.

"Not that big," Angela said. "Vince's mom, his brothers and then there's Drew, who's past eighty."

"Drew's pretty much a recluse now," Sharon said. "Last time I saw him, he was shaking so bad I thought he'd need help getting into that old truck of his. Not that anyone would necessarily feel brave enough to help him."

"I'm glad I didn't see that," Tali said. "Someone like that shouldn't be behind the wheel."

Sharon turned to Tamara. "I'm surprised you haven't heard Drew's name. He's the one who scares people. I told Jake about Drew because last time I saw him, when he was shaking so badly, was right in front of the old church."

"When?" Tamara asked.

"The day you found the sign painted on the door."

Now Tamara saw why she'd been invited to lunch. It wasn't that they wanted to get to know her, but that they wanted to get to know more about what was going on.

"He was in front of the church," Sharon continued. "Tali and I were opening up the restaurant."

"Jake didn't mention him." Tamara felt a bit flushed. Maybe Vince had more than his job connecting him to the old church. "Is Drew tall?"

"Yes. All the Frencis are tall. But if you're thinking he painted the words, not possible. Drew shakes too much. I think he has Parkinson's. If he painted the words, you'd not be able to read them."

"Was he the only one you saw?" Tamara inquired.

"That early in the morning, yes. Later on, I saw a few people who parked in your lot. Some folks still park in the old church's parking lot if the street gets crowded and Friday is one of the busiest days here at the restaurant."

"Kids play ball there in the lot. Skateboard, too," Angela added.

"Did Drew say anything to you or anybody?" Tamara asked.

"Drew doesn't talk to people—he snarls," Angela said. "It wasn't the first time he's stopped at the old building. These past few weeks, he drives by often. I told the sheriff."

"Define often," Tamara urged.

"He started driving by near the end of April. I remember because I was putting Easter decorations up and saw him. I maybe saw him once or twice a month. This month, he's driving by about every morning. Sometimes he stops."

Tamara now had a few questions to ask Vince, number one being why he hadn't mentioned his uncle's presence on her property that day two weeks ago.

"Well," Tali said. "Enough speculation. We're glad you bought the property, although I wished I'd known it was for sale. I didn't even know until recently that Lydia Griffin owned the place. Her name wasn't the one on the deed."

Angela raised an eyebrow. "How do you know that?"

Yes, Tamara thought, *how do you know that?* Although she didn't say it out loud, Tamara knew for a fact that she'd seen Lydia's name on much of the paper-work. Billy's name, though, had been on the purchase agreement and most of the other documents.

"We looked at it before we rented this place. We were thinking more a combination breakfast/lunch kind of place where we could maybe sell a few antiques. We also thought it would be a good idea to own our place of business instead of rent. We tried to make an offer—I mean, the building's just been left there to rot—but while we could find an address for the owner, a P.O. box in Colorado, no one responded to our inquiry."

"Do you remember who you wrote to?" Tamara asked.

Tali shook his head, but Sharon looked thoughtful. "I remember it wasn't Lydia. It was some sort of trust or corporation."

Vince took off work early. It wasn't that much of a hardship. He'd spent all morning at the hospital where he'd been running conduit. Then, during the afternoon, he'd started cutting out holes for electrical outlets. Just before two, Gloria Baker, the head nurse who pretty much ruled the hospital, came in, pursed her lips and then took off.

His boss, John Konrad, showed up a few minutes later. It seemed the outlets were not where the nurse wanted them. Although they were where the blueprints said they should be, it looked like the nurse outranked the project manager.

An hour of work wasted, and now tomorrow he'd be not only cutting more electrical socket holes but filling in old ones.

He clocked out in pretend disgust.

Actually, disgust had nothing to do with it. He'd been looking for an excuse to leave since noon. He wanted to check on Tamara.

Her car looked forlorn in the old church's parking lot. He parked next to it and started walking toward the front door. A mountain of garbage bags was behind the church. The front porch was swept and a new blanket already covered the bench. Vince wasn't surprised. He'd doubted Tamara knew how to take it easy. He tried to open the front door and found it was locked. He knocked.

No one answered.

Taking out his key—the one Lydia had given him to use only in case of an emergency—he let himself in while calling Tamara's name.

Still, no one answered.

The dust in the room wasn't quite as bad as the last time he'd been inside. Already much of the loose paper and junk had been carted from the main room. All that remained were the broken pews and some shattered glass in a corner.

He cleaned it up; he didn't want her to cut herself.

Afterward he continued looking for her, but she wasn't anywhere inside the church. Dread, tangible and spreading, washed down the back of Vince's neck. Opening his wallet, he found Tamara's cell phone number and dialed.

She answered on the first ring. He didn't bother with pleasantries. "Where are you?"

"I'm eating lunch at Yano's."

"I'll be right there."

"Good, the ravioli's wonderful."

It sounded as if she was chewing while she was talking. Good. Last year, when they'd walked down the aisle during Lisa's wedding, she'd been curves and power. Now, since her ordeal with the stalker, she was thin, too thin. Maybe with a bit of meat on her bones, she'd get some of the power back.

He missed it.

The bell over Yano's clanged as he walked in. He saw her before she saw him.

She didn't wear a three-piece suit today. Instead, she wore jeans. Not ragged and worn like his. A pink button-down shirt highlighted her hair. She leaned forward in her chair, legs crossed at her ankles, and was dividing her attention between whatever was on her fork and Tali Rasmussen.

They sat at a table for four, but soon another chair was added and Vince was sitting, again, way too close to Tamara. Tali was too interested in the conversation to pay attention to Vince, but Sharon raised an eyebrow. He'd eaten many meals here and, according to them, too many meals alone. They'd gone out of their way to make sure the unattached waitresses served him.

Looked as if that wouldn't be a problem for a while, judging by the look in Sharon's eye.

Angela couldn't hide a somewhat amused look. The bookstore owner was single, but quite a few years older than Vince, otherwise the Rasmussens would have had her on the short list for Vince's attention.

He'd set them straight later.

"Did you know the Rasmussens tried to buy the old church a few years ago?" Tamara asked him.

"No. As far as I knew, it was never on the market until recently."

"It wasn't," Tali said. "We just attempted to locate the owner and make an offer, but nothing ever came of it."

Sharon's eyes lit up. The legs on her chair scraped loudly against the floor and she pushed closer to the table and to Vince. "Did you know that Lydia Griffin owned it? We didn't."

Vince shifted uncomfortably. No sense denying the truth since it wasn't a secret anymore. "I knew."

Sharon put her elbows on the table and leaned forward, her eyes glistening. "So, how much property does Lydia own?" she asked.

"I never asked her. I did the yardwork for the church, for the house Lydia lived in, and for one rental property."

"I think I knew about the rental," Sharon told Tali before turning to Vince. "Are you going to be working for the son now?"

"Oh, leave Vince alone," Tali said. "Let's change the subject and get some food in his stomach." Tali looked at Vince. "The usual?"

Vince nodded and slowly sat back down.

"Men are always more likely to tell tales when their stomachs are full," Sharon joked.

"You mean you're more likely to tell tales—tall tales," Tali said, helping his wife from her chair.

Both Sharon and Angela burst out laughing. Tamara managed a giggle.

Tali and Sharon disappeared into the kitchen, and Angela went to the restroom.

Vince reached for an empty water glass and the pitcher of water.

"Do you know the name of the corporation Tali mentioned?" Tamara's innocent, laid-back expression was gone. The lawyer was back, and she'd know if he were lying.

"Yes."

"Are all her properties listed under the corporation?"

"No."

"An estimate, what percent? Half?"

"Tamara, this is none of your business."

"It's my business if someone's trying to scare me away because someone in that corporation doesn't want me owning the church."

She had a good point, he realized.

"You might as well tell me the name of the corporation," Tamara continued. "I'm going to find out anyway."

"My checks always came from the Lylo Foundation."

"Never heard of it. What else do you know?"

"Nothing. I didn't care who signed my check. I only cared that I was able to cash it. Until you came along, there was nothing suspicious about it."

She looked thoughtful. "I think I'm going to enjoy every minute of finding out all about the Lylo Foundation."

Suddenly, a scream came from the foyer.

"That's Sharon," Tamara said. "She's excitable."

Vince pushed his seat out. "Not that excitable."

The next scream came with a word—a word that had Tamara exiting her chair, too.

Fire!

SIX

Thanks to a simple glance out the door by Sharon, who knew the beginnings of a fire when she saw one, what could have been the end to Tamara's first attempt at opening her own law office turned into just a little smoke and water damage.

Tamara kicked at the soaked wood that made up her storm cellar door. "I hadn't even gotten down there to explore yet. I hope nothing was ruined."

"I don't think there's anything down there to ruin. But you're right. We need to find out. Lydia claimed going down there wasn't safe. I thought she meant structurally. Now, thanks to the water damage, we better check it out soon," Vince said. "Judging by the lock, I don't think anyone's been down there in years."

A loud *whish* sound filled the air, a siren started, cut off, and a child squealed. Then, the fire engine pulled away from the curb, taking with it not only the firemen but half the spectators.

There really hadn't been enough of a fire to draw a crowd, but the fire truck, firemen and noise couldn't be ignored.

The fire inspector still walked around. He was efficient. He tried to open the storm cellar door and frowned. He moved on—all the while entering information onto some electronic clipboard. Occasionally, he stopped to ask Vince, Tamara or one of the spectators a question.

Tamara shook her head. Everyone considered Vince the authority on the place. Before the police arrived, he knew where the hose and hookups were. He'd pretty much put out the small fire before the fire truck arrived. Then, when the questions started to fly, he knew the answers.

"The home inspector didn't say anything about structural weakness, and I'm sure he would have," Tamara said. "I read the paperwork. He said the place was a mess, but sound."

"You know, Lydia could have been feeding me a line. About that time, teenagers were breaking into the church to make out. Maybe she thought I'd spread the word that the storm cellar was dangerous."

More than likely, Vince had been the danger, as one of the teenagers making out, Tamara thought.

She was doing entirely too much thinking about that subject, and staring at his lips, too.

Must be the image of kids making out.

"I can leave it until last," she stated.

Vince shook his head. "A storm cellar has saved many a life here in Sherman. We get plenty of tornadoes. I'd hire someone to get it up to par."

"If you're my handyman, wouldn't that be your job?"

"I'll put it on my list."

Before the conversation could go anywhere else, the sheriff walked up. Jake raised an eyebrow and asked, "What are you going to work on?"

"The storm cellar," Tamara replied.

"Good idea. Nebraska gets plenty of tornadoes—"

"We're fifth in the U.S," Vince interrupted. "And Sherman is right in the tornado belt."

"Tornado belt?" Tamara asked.

"Texas, Oklahoma, Kansas, South Dakota and us," Jake answered. "We're the tornado belt. We had five tornado warnings last year, but only one touched down."

This was not something Tamara had considered when she'd put her condo on the market back in Arizona.

"Okay, I'm convinced, I'll make that storm cellar a priority," Tamara decided.

"That would be wise." Jake took a step back and turned to look at Vince. His expression went grim. "So, Vincent Frenci, I hear you arrived on the scene about the time the fire started?"

"What?" Tamara and Vince said in unison.

Tamara hadn't missed Jake's suddenly calling Vince by his full name. It was a strategic move.

It didn't work.

If anything, Vince relaxed. "You think I started the fire and then moseyed over to have lunch with Tamara while her building went up in flames?"

The sheriff didn't nod; he didn't have to.

"What about his motive?" Tamara asked.

Before Jake could answer, the fire inspector's cell phone rang.

He barked a hello and then listened. After a moment, his jaw dropped and he almost grinned.

"That man only gets that excited if he knows something," Jake said.

It was Vince who reacted the most to the fire inspector's announcement. "Drew Frenci just showed at the Sherman Hospital emergency room with second-degree burns on his hands."

* * *

Drew certainly wasn't going to die, not if the strength of his lungs was any indicator. "I tell you. I was lighting my cigarette and the whole pack just plain went up in flames!" Drew's voice carried from behind the swinging hospital doors and out into the lobby where no one dared to talk.

Jake stood just beside the swinging doors waiting for someone to tell him how his uncle was doing. In the hard yellow chair next to Vince, Tamara bent down and pulled out her cell phone. She looked sheepishly at the Please Turn Off Your Cell Phone sign posted across from them and punched a button before dropping the phone back into her purse. She then whispered, "At the restaurant, Sharon said your uncle Drew couldn't have painted the sign on the front door. She said Drew shakes too much."

"I want to tell you I'm surprised, but nothing that man does surprises me," Vince admitted. "He'd kill a mouse. He'd slash tires. Could he control the shakes enough to paint the words legibly? I don't know. Maybe. But why? I've never even heard him mention the Amhurst Church. He knows I work there, so if he was going to target me, why now? For the past ten years, he's rarely left his trailer."

"Something must be motivating him," Tamara said.

"It's just one more thing to deal with." Vince closed his eyes and leaned his head back against the hard wall of the hospital. "I should have seen this coming."

"How could you have seen this coming?"

Vince opened his eyes. "Oh, come on, Tamara. At the restaurant, I'm sure you heard all about my family. You didn't even need to ask who Drew was when the fire inspector said his name."

She bit her lower lip.

"See? And you heard Jake trying to pin all this either on me or because of me."

She had the decency to nod, but then she did the unexpected. She put her hand on top of his. "But I knew it wasn't you."

"It wasn't me, but it circles back to me."

"What do you mean?"

"I mean my mom's whole life has been trying to get out from under the thumb of that old man. And, now I'm trying to do the same thing."

She didn't respond. She just looked at him, managing to appear caring, as if *he* really mattered.

Best thing to do was shut up, keep his family life a secret. Instead, his mouth opened, like he had no control, and when she squeezed his hand, just once, very gently, the words poured out.

"Before Drew became a recluse, back when I was a teenager, I remember the VA hospital over in Omaha used to call my mom at least once a month to come get him. What Drew really wanted was to stay in the hospital, do nothing and stay medicated. The hospital's goal, at first, was to get him through detox. Pretty soon, he wore out his welcome. Not that he noticed, but we sure did. His hospital stays got shorter and shorter.

"About the same time he got the idea that someone was stealing from him and started having all his bills and checks mailed to my mom's house. Then, he accused her of stealing his money. He even got violent once and hit her. She called the police and got a restraining order. Drew stayed away for three months. They were the most peaceful months I remember.

"About ten years ago, he fell and broke his ankle. It

slowed him down. We took that to read 'calmed' him down. We were wrong."

"I'd say you weren't wrong. I mean, so far he hasn't managed to scare me off."

Yet, Vince thought. *Drew hasn't scared you off yet.*

"This is not your fault," Tamara said. "You cannot control him."

"No, but he sure seems to control us. To this day, most of his bills are still mailed to my mom's house, and she winds up paying some of them because she'd rather spend the money than face him."

What Vince didn't say was that he wound up paying most of them, not his mother, because she didn't have the money.

"So, if Drew was such a threat, all those years, why didn't your mother just pack everyone up and move?"

Vince had his ideas, and the one that topped the list made no sense. He believed that deep down, his mother still thought her husband, Vince's father, might come home and she didn't want to risk leaving Sherman.

He couldn't tell Tamara that—she'd only ask more questions. He opened his mouth to change the subject, but before a single word came out, from behind the doors separating the waiting room from the emergency room they heard more of Drew's angry yelling. "Come near me with that needle, and it will be the last shot you give!"

Jake hurried from his spot against the wall. He disappeared through the swinging door.

Vince was right behind.

Tamara stood. This wasn't her case, and Drew wasn't family, so she didn't follow.

Suddenly a woman and man entered the waiting room

and started toward the nurse on duty. But then Darren, Vince's brother, changed course and headed for Tamara.

"Mom, this is Tamara."

Vince's mother didn't much look like him. For one thing, she wasn't tall. For another, Tamara wasn't sure what her real hair color was, but based on eyebrow color and complexion, it wasn't black. "What's Drew done now?" she asked.

Tamara stood. "Mrs. Frenci, it looks as though Drew seriously burned himself trying to set a fire, but we're not sure. Vince just went to see. He should be out in a minute."

Even with a pinched expression, Vince's mother didn't look old enough to be his mother. She looked only slightly older than the man standing next to her.

"It's Billingsby now," Vince's mother said. "I briefly remarried. You can call me Debbie. Where did he try to set the fire and why?"

"He tried to burn my building, and we don't know why."

Vince's brother was a bit more to the point. "How much trouble is Drew in?"

"I don't really know," Tamara admitted, sitting back down. "Right now they're just worried about the burns on his hands."

"You recently bought the old church, right? Will you press charges?" Debbie said.

"I may not have to. If the fire marshal finds proof, it will be out of my hands."

Debbie looked at the swinging door, looked at her son and then, with a sigh, sat down next to Tamara. She gripped the arms of the chair with fingers so tense they resembled claws.

"Mom, it will be okay." Darren didn't sit down. He

looked like he wanted to be anywhere but standing in the middle of a hospital waiting room while his uncle shouted obscenities so loudly that they all had to raise their voices to speak over the noise. "You want me to go check?"

"I doubt they'll let you in," Tamara said. "Both Vince and the sheriff are in there. Hospitals seldom allow more than two visitors at a time."

"He'd just cuss at us anyway," Debbie said.

The front doors opened again. This time it wasn't a Frenci. It was Lisa, looking flushed.

"Are you all right?" she asked Tamara. "I had to find out on the five-o'clock news that somebody tried to burn down your building. I've called your cell phone twice. Why aren't you answering? Finally, I called Angela, and she said she thought you'd come here, and that somehow you've managed to annoy Drew Frenci."

As if proving a point, Drew managed to break a sound barrier or two.

Lisa raised an eyebrow. "Is he going to be okay?"

"My uncle is never okay," Darren said.

"Let's just hope Drew's okay enough to go to jail," Debbie muttered.

Darren's grin disappeared. "He should go to jail whether he's okay or not."

Tamara had heard such talk from relatives more times than she wanted to count—during depositions, in the courtroom, on the witness stand. There came a time when career criminals lost even their most devoted family members. For some, it was a rude awakening. For others, it didn't even inspire a blink.

It sounded like in his old age, Drew was more mentally ill than criminal. It also sounded like Drew didn't have any devoted family members left.

Another torrent of words erupted from the emergency room. Lisa hugged herself, her pregnancy making her appear more vulnerable than usual.

"Look—" Tamara started, thinking she'd suggest Lisa go home and wait by the phone.

Lisa, however, had other ideas. "Maybe we should say a prayer."

"What?" Vince's brother almost snarled.

"Darren!" Debbie scolded. Then, turning to Lisa, she said in a subdued voice. "It's a little too late for prayers, at least on Drew's account."

Almost as if cued, silence fell. After a full half hour listening to a wild man's ranting, the lack of noise was almost tangible.

"Never too late," Lisa said. She bowed her head and started, "Dear Lord…"

Tamara was too surprised to protest.

Debbie, for all that she'd claimed it too late, went ahead and bowed.

Darren and Tamara exchanged looks but kept quiet as Lisa continued, "…an elderly man in more pain than we can imagine…"

Tamara got the feeling Lisa wasn't talking about Drew's burns.

Watching Debbie, Tamara noticed how her fingers relaxed at just the moment Lisa uttered, "…and be with both the hospital staff and Drew's family as they…" Vince's mother was actually listening to Lisa's words.

"What will most likely happen to Drew?" Debbie asked after Lisa said *Amen.* "I mean, you're a lawyer, you should know."

"Mom," Darren said. "She's not the right lawyer to ask. Drew tried to burn down her office."

"No, you can ask. I do know that if he set the fire, and he's found competent, he'll stand trial for arson."

Vince chose that moment to return. He hugged his mother and nodded at his brother. "Drew's competent all right. He knows exactly what he's done. He's madder than spit that it didn't work."

"Your girlfriend's lucky," Vince's brother said. "A few years ago, Drew not only would have managed to burn the church down but he'd have gotten away with it."

Tamara opened her mouth to protest, but Vince didn't even seem to notice his brother's assumption about her position in his life.

"You got that right, Darren," Vince said. "Looks like he set the garbage bags on fire and then as he was turning to go he tripped on one. Went right into the fire and had a hard time getting up. Funny thing is, he fell on the fire and pretty much put it out, which is why you don't have more damage."

"Why'd he do it?" Tamara asked.

Vince shook his head. "All he'll say is he needs to keep Lydia safe."

"Lydia? Lydia Griffin?" Vince's mom sounded surprised. "What does she have to do with this?"

"If you knew," Vince said, "you'd be the star witness."

"I will never understand how that man's mind works," Debbie almost spit. "How long will he be in the hospital?"

"It's going to be a while," Jake said, joining them. He looked a bit frazzled. Darren stepped back, almost as if he were preconditioned to avoid cops.

Jake continued. "The doctors are concerned about Drew's age and how severely he was burned."

"He's not going to be able to care for himself when he's released from the hospital," Debbie said morosely.

"When he's released from the hospital," Jake said, "he'll be booked into jail." He looked at Tamara. "Do me a favor, file a report today."

Debbie looked relieved, and suddenly Tamara realized that Debbie's fear was not that Drew would go to jail but that he wouldn't.

SEVEN

"We need you to come down to the station to fill out some paperwork," Jake told Tamara.

"I'll take you there," Vince said.

For the second time, Lisa raised an eyebrow.

"Don't read anything into it, sis," Tamara warned. "Everything just happened so fast. When we heard that Drew was in the emergency room, I jumped into Vince's truck and we headed over."

Lisa simply smiled.

A nurse called Debbie and the whole family went to confer with what looked like a doctor. After about five minutes, Vince came back. "We can go now," he said to Tamara. "Mom and Darren are here. Mom is Drew's power of attorney. Nothing more I can really do. Plus, the doctors just gave Drew a shot of morphine. He's already out."

After only two steps toward the door, Tamara felt Vince's hand on the small of her back. It startled her enough to make her turn around. Vince was looking back, with a worried expression, at his mother and brother.

He wasn't even aware that he was touching her.

It was automatic.

So was his opening the door for her. It was on the tip of her tongue to protest, but he was still looking back through the glass doors of the hospital waiting room where his mother and brother remained.

"Vince, why don't you stay here with your family? I can walk over to the police station. It's only about five minutes away."

He tore his gaze away from the hospital door and shook his head as he opened the door of his truck for her. "No, the sheriff's already told me he needs to talk to me. Looks like you have a partner whether you want one or not." Vince gently closed the passenger's-side door and hurried around to the other side. He climbed in and started the engine.

On the ride to the hospital, she really hadn't paid any attention to his vehicle. She'd been thinking about the fire.

Now, she had time. His truck wasn't new. It was probably decades old. For a construction guy, the truck was amazingly clean. He hadn't pushed things off the seat to make room for her. She hadn't maneuvered her feet between tools and fast-food bags. There was a gearshift on the steering mechanism. The leather seats were cracked.

"Since the window won't roll down, how about turning on the air conditioner?" she suggested.

"Truck didn't come with air-conditioning. Of course, if you plan on being a passenger now and then, I might fix the window."

Did she plan on being a passenger now and then? Maybe if her life ever settled down.

"How about the radio? Does it work?" she asked.

He shook his head. "I'll fix that for you, too, but don't think you're going to get to listen to country."

"What's wrong with country?"

"Just about everything," he retorted.

"Well, I like country."

He laughed. "I guess if you plan on being a passenger now and then, I'll have to learn to suffer."

Funny how just a few words could make a woman suddenly rethink a relationship. Just in case she needed the option, she said, "I think you need to fix the window and the radio."

He grinned. "Not to worry. I was planning to do it anyway. Restoring this baby is my side passion. Not that I've had much time—" he patted the dashboard "—to work on her lately. I'm too busy taking care of you."

"Oh, right," she teased. "I've been back in town for all of two days."

"And," Vince said as he parked in front of the police station, "look at how much trouble you've gotten in."

"Me," she squeaked. "What about you?"

"I'm not trouble."

"No, but it sounds like your uncle Drew is."

Vince sobered. His fingers tightened on the steering wheel. "We can't joke when it comes to Uncle Drew. He's like a tornado. You never know when he's going to strike."

"Why'd he do it? He doesn't even know me."

Vince shook his head. "It's crazy. All he'll say is he did it to keep Lydia safe."

"She's still in the nursing home. Her son's been flying back and forth taking care of her. I doubt she even knows Billy sold the church. How would preventing me from buying the church keep her safe?" Tamara raised an eyebrow. "Were he and Lydia good friends? Does he think Billy was acting without his mother's best interest in mind?"

The thought of his uncle acting in someone else's best interest almost made Vince laugh. "No, I don't think he was trying to help Lydia because he distrusted Billy. Honestly, I don't know what my uncle was thinking and he's not saying. They weren't friends, at least not that I know of. My uncle doesn't have any friends. I asked my mother if she had any ideas. She said she thought she'd heard something about them going together when they were young, but she didn't move to Sherman until after she married my dad. She only knows so much of the Frenci history."

"Do you remember your dad saying anything?"

"No," he said curtly.

"I'm sorry," Tamara said softly. To his relief, she didn't ask questions.

"Are you going to press charges? Drew's no stranger to being behind bars, but at his age, I'm not sure how he'd handle it. He's got a bad heart."

"I'm not going to press charges. I'll file a report, for insurance purposes, but that's all."

"I'm not sure if I need to tell you you're crazy or if I need to thank you. I'm not going to lie. Drew's trouble with a capital *T,* and the fact that he's older than dirt doesn't make him any less dangerous. He can manipulate people. He's made my mother's life a nightmare in some ways. And granted, his attempt to start a fire didn't work, but he's the kind of man who will try something like that. What if he gets some harebrained idea, tries it and it works? You could get hurt."

She wanted to say she could take care of herself, but lately she didn't feel that way. Always there was the thought that maybe something more was out there. She wasn't quite sure what more was.

Vince shook his head, completely unaware of the maelstrom he'd stirred up. "I've been dealing with Drew most of my life. I don't understand him, but he's blood."

"I understand."

"I don't think you do. By not pressing charges, you've put yourself at risk. I feel partly responsible. If you don't want to hire me because of Uncle Drew, I completely understand."

"Okay."

"Okay, what? You're not hiring me?" He wasn't quite sure what he'd do, say, if she changed her mind, because as long as Drew had a vendetta against her, he intended to watch over her.

"Okay, I'm not pressing charges and okay, you're hired."

"That's it?" Vince tried not to sound doubtful, but the woman was a lawyer, after all. Surely there were a half-dozen laws she should be shouting about.

"You're not acting at all like I expected."

"How did you expect me to act? Not that I approve of his tactics, but it's actually kind of gallant, your uncle wanting to take care of Lydia."

Nope, the Frenci men didn't fall into the gallant category. Especially Drew.

What Vince really wanted to know was why was Drew acting "gallant" now? Lydia Griffin had been in Sherman for decades.

Vince knew his uncle enough to suspect that taking care of Lydia meant taking care of Tamara, and it wasn't the good kind of taking care.

Drew didn't do the good kind, *ever.*

* * *

The Sherman Police Station was located right next to Sherman High School. Not bad planning, Tamara thought as Vince jumped out and came around to open her door.

They went up the three steps that led to the station's front door. The front desk officer stood up, and Vince and Tamara were separated. She imagined that Vince would be answering "Uncle Drew" questions. She, on the other hand, wound up filing a criminal intent complaint for insurance purposes. It took all of ten minutes.

Vince wasn't ready to go for another half hour. It gave Tamara time to walk around the lobby of the police station. While the dispatcher appeared to pay her no mind, Tamara knew the woman watched her every move. No surprise. The front of the station was mainly windows. The view wasn't that impressive. Look to the left and there was an old movie theater. Look straight ahead and there was the high school. Look to the right and there was the only other lawyer's office in town.

Tamara needed to introduce herself soon. The thought brought a grin. Until she had come to town, the man had had a monopoly.

The lobby's reception area was empty. Apparently Monday evenings were slow in Sherman. Tamara walked past the public restrooms and studied some of the stuff on the walls. A bulletin board held most wanted listings. Next to that were the photos. Jake was there, labeled as acting sheriff. Tamara glanced at his citations and a few newspaper articles, framed, giving him accolades. Next to Jake's photo was his father's. One newspaper article was enlarged. Tamara quickly read, feeling a heart-tug of sympathy. Too many good cops died in the line of duty while too many rights were given to the criminals they fought. Tamara didn't know Jake's age, so she couldn't do the math, but she could guess that Jake had still been in school when his father died.

Jake's grandfather's photo was next. Most of the accolades about Jasper had to do with his work with children. He'd coached baseball, started a youth center and even a junior police academy. The man was ahead of his time there.

"Is Jasper still alive?" Tamara asked the dispatcher.

"Yes." The woman looked up at Tamara, and then back down at the paperwork on her desk. Before Tamara could assure the woman she was just curious, nothing else, Vince came into the waiting room. "Well, that was interesting. What you filled out is merely an accusation. Until more proof is determined, Drew's presumed innocent."

"It's the way our law works. We don't want to make a mistake, accidentally indict the wrong man. You know, we never considered that perhaps Drew saw the fire and fell while trying to put it out."

The dispatcher chuckled.

"Let's go," Vince suggested. "I'm never comfortable in police stations."

When they were back in the front seat of Vince's truck, Tamara started to talk, but Vince just shook his head.

They made it to the church in ten minutes. Yellow tape still cordoned off the area behind the church where Tamara had stacked garbage bags.

"The front door's open," Vince said.

"What?"

Sure enough, the door was open.

"You stay here," Vince ordered. He jumped out of the truck. By the time she had one foot on the ground, he was inside the building.

Where were the spectators now? Or even a few pedestrians or the nosy neighbors? The bookstore next door was closed up, but Yano's was bustling and music spilled into the street.

She followed Vince to the porch and peered in the door. She could hear someone running up the stairs to the attic. She assumed it was Vince, but the thought that it could be someone else made her breath catch.

She knew better than to follow him in. If someone dangerous was inside, she'd be a distraction. She ran back to the truck and scooted in through the still open passenger's-side door. Her purse was on the seat, her cell phone right on top.

She dialed 911 and waited.

Just as she finished giving the details, Vince came to the door.

"You can come in now!" he shouted.

"I called the sheriff. He's on his way back."

"Good, he'll want to see this."

"Do I want to see this?"

"Probably not."

She grabbed her purse and headed for Vince. He held the door. She only needed to take one step into the main room to see the destruction. This morning she'd cleared the room except for the damaged pews and some broken glass in the corner. While she'd been at the hospital and then the station, someone had poured white flour everywhere. They'd also thrown something doughy at the walls.

"Oven rolls," Vince explained. "Kids used to throw them at car windows. They explode really good."

Tamara decided not to ask him how he knew this.

Beside the erratic dough art, the walls, dull white, were now dull white highlighted with black spray paint and gang symbols, although not any gang symbols she recognized.

"What does the rest of the place look like?"

"More flour and biscuits, but this is the only room with the graffiti."

"I'm surprised no one noticed or heard anything," Tamara said.

"Whoever did this entered through a kitchen window. They exited from the front, probably looking out the window to make sure no one was around. Then, they jumped off the side of the porch and headed around back. Pretty easy. Plus, painting and throwing flour around doesn't make much noise."

"It probably only took them about thirty minutes to do," Tamara said mournfully. "It will take about thirty hours to repair."

Vince moved up next to her, so close she could feel his arm brush against hers. "Once we paint, and get rid of the flour, you'll forget all about this vandalism. I'm not going to say it's easily fixed, but it's fixable."

Every fiber of Tamara's being was yelling for her to run. Yet, this was obviously not the work of William Massey. It also wasn't Drew.

If she ran away now, would she know when to stop running?

"I left some broken glass in the corner this morning. It's gone. I don't suppose that means anything," she said.

"I cleaned it up when I first looked for you before I called your cell phone and discovered you were at Yano's."

Lunch seemed a long time ago. So did Vince's good mood in the truck before they arrived at the police station.

"I guess we'll be giving more statements to the police," Vince said.

"And they'll be going door-to-door trying to find out if anyone saw something." Tamara shivered. "I'm trying not to let this scare me, but it does."

"It should!" Vince snapped. "It should scare you into renting a nice office someplace else. Isn't there a thirty-day grace period where you can walk away from the deal?"

She *could* get out of the sale. She was a lawyer and knew just where the weakness in the contract was.

But what if something like this happened at the next place, and the next?

She could stick it out a bit longer, make a stand, try to deal with the fear. She took out her phone, quickly called her insurance company and then said, "I still like the building. I like the location and I like the potential."

Tamara felt only slightly better. She couldn't remember the last time she'd walked away from an opportunity to improve her life.

Even with her fiancé, she hadn't walked away. He had, after seven years, seven long years. They'd dated in college, graduated together and worked together. They were alike, both driven. Oh, she was the one who handed the ring back, but he was the one who broke faith when he didn't believe her about William Massey until it was too late. And she'd always wonder if he put off believing her because of convenience.

"This building has the potential to get you killed," Vince said gently. Somehow, hearing his voice, the tremor in his words, made Tamara realize just how much her heart wanted to believe that he cared. No, not possible.

"It's not the building," Tamara protested, "it's who-ever..." Her words tapered off.

"I wondered how much thought you'd given to what's just happened."

She'd given it plenty of thought. And she was working at making herself angry instead of scared. Anger was good. In this case, it would keep her on her toes. Fear never solved any problem.

"So," she said, "since there's no way Drew did this, do you have any idea who might be working with your uncle?"

The sheriff didn't send an underling, which let Tamara know just how seriously he was taking the break-in. He came with two detectives in tow. Now, along with the outside, the inside of the church, too, was cordoned off.

"I'm sorry," Jake said as he watched one of the detectives dust the front door for fingerprints. "I know you wanted to get to work and that you have a personal deadline, but it's probably going to be a few days before we can let you in."

"Do you have any idea who could have done this?" Tamara asked. "I mean, we know it's not Drew. Any chance this truly was teenagers having fun?"

Jake shook his head. "This was the work of one person. The rage was directed at you." He stared at Vince hard. "Any chance you know?"

"No chance at all. I'm still trying to come to terms with Drew's involvement."

"Darren didn't look too happy at the hospital today," Jake remarked.

"Well," Vince said snidely, "as you know, happiness is not a Frenci family trait."

"Where's Mickey?" Jake asked. "He still in the Nebraska State Penitentiary?"

"You know he is."

"Jimmy staying out of trouble?"

Vince's lips were pressed together so tightly that the surrounding skin was almost white. "Jimmy's going to be a senior this upcoming year. He might even be the first Frenci to go to college."

"He's not really a Frenci," Jake said.

"Look—" Vince took a menacing step toward Jake.

Tamara stepped in between. "What about the gang symbols on the wall?" she asked.

The look Jake gave her said he was well aware of why she'd interrupted. What she couldn't tell was whether he was pleased or not.

Vince certainly wasn't pleased.

"They're not gang symbols," Jake said. "Those are some sort of Japanese symbols. I've had the graffiti squad at the high school more than once painting over walls and fences."

"That should help us figure out who the culprit is, don't you think?" Tamara asked.

"Yes, the symbols point to a kid, but that doesn't make my job any easier," Jake said. "It's not just high school and junior high kids into this anime or manga stuff. The grade school kids are just as devoted and just as talented and getting just as destructive."

For the next twenty minutes, Tamara's job was to make sure nothing was missing. Since she had no real belongings in the church, it was an easy assessment. Then, Jake and the detectives left and Vince watched as she locked the building.

"You want me to follow you home?" Vince asked.

"No, I'll be fine. I know you want to get back to the hospital."

He waited until she got in her car, started the engine, and drove off, before he got on his way.

One of the town's bad boys definitely had a gallant streak.

Even with a day that entailed some of the hardest physical labor she had ever engaged in, even with a day that came with someone trying to burn down her office and ended with someone intent on vandalizing her property, Tamara smiled as she drove to her apartment.

She didn't smile a half hour later when she was sat down at her tiny kitchen table, a bowl of soup in front of her, and started checking her cell phone messages between spoonfuls.

Tamara had three messages—two were from Lisa. Both were frantic—*"Where are you?"* and *"What's happening?"*

Message number three came from a restricted number. Tamara listened to the message two times before her trembling hand set the cell phone on the table.

Looked like right now wasn't a safe time.

Drew Frenci had been in the hospital's emergency room during the time the third call came in, so it wasn't his guttural message on her voice mail.

"You can leave the old church by choice or you can leave it by a body bag. This isn't over, lady."

EIGHT

Hospital hallways always appeared eerily scant at five in the morning. Vince stopped by his uncle's room before starting work. Leaning against the door frame, he stared as Drew snored. Drew's hands were so heavily bandaged that Vince wondered if Drew would be able to lift them.

Even in sleep, Drew shook.

A tiny shard of sympathy appeared in Vince's heart. Then, Vince pushed it away. How had Drew ever considered he could set a building on fire and get away with it?

Watching Drew's gnarled fingers as they trembled, Vince knew that Drew hadn't painted the message on Tamara's door. The culprit from last night must have been responsible for that crime. The slashed tires? Vince wasn't sure if Drew had the strength. Drew, however, could have killed the mouse. And, based on the lettering and holes in the handwritten warning, Drew might be behind that warning.

The sheriff would figure it out, Vince had no doubt, but Jake Ramsey was a bit too one-sided for Vince's peace of mind. Drew *was* guilty. But so was someone else and it didn't necessarily have to be a Frenci.

"You going to stand there all morning?" Nurse Gloria Baker stepped into the room. She walked over to Drew and took a clipboard from the end of the bed. Looking up, she met Vince's eyes. "He's not doing well."

Silently, Vince backed out of the room and headed down the hall. He was working alone today. His boss, John Konrad, would be off and on site all day. If something went wrong, he'd be dealing with Gloria. Well, if anyone would know where the electrical sockets should go in a patient's room, it would be the charge nurse who used the facility almost every day.

He started by putting the electrical sockets where they "should" go. When he finished with that, he started covering up yesterday's mistakes.

"We have patients who are waiting for this room!" Gloria said. She stood in the doorway, pencil behind her ear, stethoscope in hand and a scowl on her face.

"Call my supervisor," Vince said easily. "Yesterday I was only following the specs I was given."

Her lips pursed together. She clearly was interested in something more than this-construction-project-is-taking-too-much-time talk.

"I've gone over Drew's files," she said. "Is there anything, any medication, any history, that we might not have listed on his medical history?"

"I don't know about medication," Vince admitted. "But we all wonder why he shakes so much. We know better than to ask, and he's not willing to tell. That started about three years ago. As for his language, actions and bad disposition, near as I can tell, he was born that way."

She didn't look surprised. "His regular doctor died more than five years ago. There's nothing to indicate he's seen somebody new."

"Ma'am, I can't help you. My mother will probably stop by later and chances are she knows more."

Gloria nodded. "I'll tell the doctor."

Vince checked his watch. Almost noon, and he'd only accomplished about half of what he'd set out to do.

"You stop by to see your uncle today?" The voice interrupting him this time was just as gruff as the nurse's, but it wasn't female.

Vince's fingers tightened on the screwdriver. He'd seen the sheriff more the past couple of weeks than he was comfortable with. And the little byplay last night, with the sheriff letting Tamara know that Drew wasn't the only Frenci who knew the inside of a jail cell, still rubbed Vince raw.

"I stopped in his room this morning," Vince said. "Just after five. He was asleep."

"And you haven't been by since?" Jake walked into the room, checked out what Vince was doing.

"No, I'm on the clock."

"Since when has that stopped you?"

"I'm scared of Nurse Baker," Vince admitted.

Jake laughed. It was a full-out laugh. It almost made Vince see the man as human. It also reminded Vince that, for once, he and the law were on the same side— keeping Tamara safe.

Jake finally stopped laughing. "Gloria takes her job seriously."

"You're on a first-name basis with her?" Vince asked. It figured.

"Her dad and my grandfather were friends. Gloria Baker may wear a nurse's uniform but, believe me, she runs the hospital and has for years." Jake walked into the room and sat in the only chair. "Did Drew say anything to you, either yesterday or before that, that I need to know about?"

"Like what?"

"You tell me."

"Before yesterday, all Drew did was cuss at me while I cleared out his yard. And I didn't talk to Drew at all yesterday."

The sheriff took a small notebook from his shirt pocket and wrote something down. "You make any phone calls to Drew yesterday?"

"No."

"Not to his landline or to his cell?"

"Uncle Drew doesn't have a cell phone. He's too cheap."

"You sure about that?"

Okay, the sheriff had Vince's attention and was going somewhere with this line of questioning. Vince stood and leaned against the wall. "Just say what you want to say, Sheriff."

"You got a cell phone, Vince?"

"I do."

"May I see it?"

"Do you have a warrant?"

"No, but I can get one. Do I need to?"

Vince pulled his cell phone from his belt and tossed it to the sheriff.

While Jake played with the buttons, Gloria Baker peeked in the room and then stood for a moment watching.

"Jake, if you cause him to take longer to finish this room, I'll make sure the next time you're brought to my emergency room isn't a pleasant experience." The look she shot Jake made Vince think maybe she should be sheriff.

"Understood, ma'am," Jake said. He tossed the

phone back to Vince and asked, "This the only cell phone you have?"

"Who needs two?"

"This is your personal cell. Has Konrad issued you one?"

Vince snorted.

"Well," Jake continued, "you haven't dialed or received any calls from your uncle's cell phone. Of course, I knew that already since the subpoena got me a list of his phone's activities. Hmm, why wouldn't you know your uncle's cell phone number?"

"Because like I said, I don't believe he has a cell phone."

"He's had one for three years."

"That makes no sense. My uncle's a tightwad. He wouldn't pay for something he wasn't using."

"Phone bill is paid automatically from his checking account."

"Not only is my uncle a tightwad, but why would he need a cell phone when he rarely leaves his trailer? Does it have something to do with the fire?"

"That's what I want to know. I'm guessing you haven't spoken to Tamara since yesterday."

"No, after you and your men questioned us about the vandalism inside the church, we locked the building and left. Then I came back here and sat with my mother while she stayed with Drew. At just after nine, I went home. Four in the morning comes mighty quick. I needed some sleep."

"Well, when Tamara got to her apartment last evening, she had a message on her cell phone. It basically told her if she didn't give up remodeling the old church, she could expect to give up something a bit more important, like her life."

Vince closed his eyes. He'd messed up. He should

have called her, checked up on her, but he'd stopped at a fast-food joint, gone home, eaten and fallen into bed.

"You think my uncle called her before he set the fire?"

"I wish. Then we'd still be sitting pretty with our suspect in custody. But the call came in right about the time your uncle was teaching Gloria a few words she didn't already know."

"So, somebody has my uncle's cell phone," Vince said. "And that somebody is just as unhappy with Tamara as my uncle is."

Tamara rolled out of bed at noon.

She hadn't slept until noon since...

Maybe she'd never slept that late.

Well, she didn't have that much to do. Still clad in her pink cotton pajamas, she dialed her Realtor back in Phoenix.

It was only after she learned that no one had even looked at her condo that she briefly considered heading back to Phoenix.

A not-so-safe big city.

Tamara, feeling somewhat shaky, called the local police station next, asked for Jake and got someone else. No, the female officer didn't know if they'd managed a trace on the phone call, but, yes, the officer did know that the sheriff didn't want Tamara on the ground floor of the church or outside along the back where the fire had started.

She slipped into brown slacks and a beige shirt, topped by a brown sweater, and was standing in her tiny kitchen, trying to decide what to do next, when her cell phone chimed.

The sheriff sounded busy. "I hear you needed to talk to me."

"I did. Did you find out anything about the caller?"

He was silent for a moment, then said. "We traced the call to Drew Frenci's cell phone. Only, as you know, Drew didn't make the call. As far as I know, most people, including family, didn't even know he had a cell phone. In the past three years—which is how long he's had the phone—he's made maybe two or three calls a month, until this past month. He's made about twenty. Some are to Debbie Frenci's house. She says he calls, asks for money and such. All the rest are to or from a local pay phone."

"Where is it?" Tamara asked.

"At the grocery store just down the street from your church."

"And was there a phone call made yesterday about the time the fire was set?"

Jake chuckled, but it was the kind of chuckle that denoted resignation rather than humor. "You're more comfortable as the lawyer than as the victim. Tamara, this isn't someone you're defending. The crimes are aimed at you. You need to be careful."

"I will be." She took a deep breath. In some ways, the question she was about to ask scared her more than anything. If said yes, it meant a six-month ordeal was far from over. If he said no… She asked anyway, "So, it looks like William Massey's not involved?"

"At this point," Jake said, "I'm not discounting anyone, but we're sure not finding a connection between Drew Frenci and Massey. Last time Drew was in prison, Massey was only fourteen. Plus, near as we can tell Drew's never been to Arizona nor has Massey ever been to Nebraska. Take some advice. Until we figure out what's going on, stay away from the church for the next couple of days."

"Why?"

"Because someone is still out there who thinks you're a threat. You need to let us find out who."

"That person can get to me whether I'm in my apartment or at the church," Tamara reasoned.

"But so far," Jake countered, "the only place where physical damage has been done is the church. If I were you, I'd rethink the investment. It's not worth your life."

Tamara sat down at the table. Jake was right about one thing. No building was worth her life. But when she looked at it, she could envision herself running a successful practice. She could almost see the "Tamara" she'd planned her whole life to be.

If she ran scared, everyone would remember her as the lawyer who had been spooked by a criminal, not once but twice.

Not the best way to start a practice.

Somehow keeping the old church and turning it into a law office had become the lifeline that represented Tamara rebuilding her life.

She was scared to move forward and scared to turn back, so she was standing still.

"The tires were slashed in front of my apartment," Tamara said. "So, whoever this is knows where I live. I'm no safer here. Right now I'm going to take it easy, be wary, but I'm not willing to throw in the towel. I know I'm not allowed in the main room, but can I work in the attic?"

"I'll call the CSI technician and tell him you're coming. If he says okay, you're good to go. I expect he'll be there on the premises for a good deal of the afternoon," Jake said. "Do try to keep him aware of what you're doing. Maybe you'll actually make it through a day without drama."

Tamara said goodbye and hung up the phone.

Make it through a day without drama. She certainly wanted to, because it was no fun starring in a drama she hadn't created.

It was time for this drama to come to an end. And, just like in Phoenix, she'd have to do her fair share of investigating.

She went through her manila folders until she found the one labeled Business. In it were copies and originals of all the transactions between her and Billy Griffin.

He lived in Denver with his wife. He had two grown daughters, both married with children. He'd been flying back and forth to take care of his mother. His name was on the sales agreement and on a few other documents. She looked at the dates time-stamped on the documents. Looked as if Billy's name had been added within the past two years.

Billy's work number was on a business card clipped to one of the sales documents. He managed a restaurant. Tamara dialed the number and got a cashier. The girl laughed. Seemed Billy Griffin had quit two days ago, no notice.

Okay, that was a temporary delay.

And an interesting one.

Taking a blank yellow legal pad, Tamara started jotting down ideas. For one, besides finding out where Billy was now, she needed to find out whose name had been on the deed before Billy's.

Had Lydia's name appeared or had Lylo always been documented?

Or someone else?

She decided to call the title company. They agreed to fax her the paperwork for the church property. She then set up her laptop and searched the Internet for any information about Lylo. After ten minutes exploring different search engines, she didn't find a single corporation by that name, but discovered that Lylo was a fairly common last name.

Her next move was to call her sister Lisa, but there was no answer.

Tamara pushed a button on her cell phone again, to another number on speed dial.

Vince answered after just one ring.

"Is Lydia in a retirement home, assisted living, or what?"

"Hello to you, too," Vince said. "Last I heard she was in a nursing home."

"And Sherman has one of those?" Tamara reached for the phone book.

"Yes," Vince said. "It's right next to your sister's church. You want to tell me about this phone call you got last night?"

"Good news travels fast in these parts," Tamara said more flippantly than she meant to. "At least we know it wasn't Drew. So, maybe your family isn't to blame."

"If someone has Drew's phone, my family is probably to blame," Vince said wearily.

"I don't know," Tamara said doubtfully. "There are plenty of threads in this mystery that don't point to your family. The Lylo Foundation for one. Which leads me to what I'm going to do next. I'm going to call the nursing home and see if Lydia's still a patient. Then, I'm either going to go visit her or I'm going to go work on the attic."

"I get off in thirty minutes. Call me and tell me which one, and I'll come help."

"I can handle Lydia alone."

"I've been working alongside Lydia for more than a decade. She'll say things to me she would never say to you."

"That's called a winning argument," Tamara said. "I'll let you know what I'm doing as soon as I know what I'm doing."

The nursing home wouldn't give out information about Lydia, but Tamara got the very strong hint that the elderly woman wasn't up to visitors.

Twenty minutes later, Tamara stood in the doorway of her building and watched what looked to be a very capable CSI go about his work.

"Find anything?" she asked, peeking in the open front door.

"Don't touch anything" was the only response.

She used the back door and climbed to the attic. Today, she'd empty it out. Tomorrow, she'd scrub. Then, she'd start painting. She'd do hunter-green paint for the walls and emphasize with a cream border.

She set her purse on the desk and headed down to her car to get garbage bags.

Vince showed up ten minutes into her cleaning frenzy. "You didn't call," he accused.

"Lydia can't have visitors, and I meant to call when I got here, but I forgot."

He'd obviously come straight from work. His gray-and-white-striped shirt had Frenci embroidered on the breast. His gray pants were already slightly dusty with a white residue. He wore brown boots with steel toes. Once again, the room looked smaller just because he was in it.

"Lawyers never forget," he said.

"They do when they get really involved in a case."

"You don't have any cases yet," Vince reasoned.

"Sure I do. I have my own case, and I have this room."

Vince looked at her for a few moments, the same look Jake gave her last night when he stopped by to listen to her cell phone message.

"I'll start over here." He motioned toward one of the walls. Some plaster had fallen from the roof. There were a few boxes underneath. Somewhere, somehow, there'd been water damage.

"Did you think about calling me last night?" he asked after a few minutes.

She blew a lock of hair that had fallen down her cheek and over her nose and looked at him.

"What could you have done? Listened to the message and gotten angry? I called the police. Jake came over and listened to the message and got angry."

"Do you still have the message on your phone?"

He wasn't going to rest until he heard the message. She straightened, went to her purse, took out the phone and pushed a few buttons. Then she handed him her phone and watched his face.

He never changed expressions.

He listened to the message three times. "I don't recognize the voice, but it sounds like somebody was purposely talking in a guttural voice."

"I couldn't tell if it was someone young or old," Tamara admitted.

"Didn't sound female," Vince said. "No, definitely male."

Tamara snapped her finger. "That's what I should have asked the CSI guy downstairs. Maybe he's already figured out what the graffiti meant."

"I'll go ask."

She shadowed Vince down the stairs and to the front porch, but the door was shut and locked, and the cordon tape in place.

"Guess they'll tell us when they're ready," he said.

"Or in a little while, I'll make a phone call." Tamara was never one to wait.

They headed back upstairs, Vince went back to gathering trash and Tamara opened the door to the closet. Three hangers and a lot of dust took up little space.

"This is a decent-size closet," she said. "When I was young, maybe in first or second grade, we lived in a house that had a closet like this. Maybe a bit bigger. My sister Sheila and I made it into our playhouse."

"You had a playhouse?"

"Hey, I was six!" Tamara ducked her head and went into the closet. A moment later, she exited, found a flashlight and then went back. To the left, it went out three feet. To the right, only about one.

"What did Lisa do while you and Sheila played house?" Vince asked.

"Lisa's the baby. She was either asleep in her crib or getting in our way." Tamara laughed at the memory. "I guess maybe that is when I first showed signs of my future lawyering skills. Sheila would always try to scare Lisa away, and I always tried to reason with Lisa."

"Sheila's the middle sister?"

"Yes, the only one staying near Mom. She's a writer. She'd like to be the next *New York Times* bestseller, but so far she makes her living teaching part-time, writing magazine pieces and how-to manuals and stuff." Tamara felt along the top shelf and made a face at the amount of dust she got on her hand. "I'm thinking that those boxes you're looking at came from in here. There's evidence of water damage." She sneezed and then, as her foot connected with something soft, she moved clumsily to the left. Before she could catch her breath, the flashlight dropped to the floor and rolled away. Its light flickered and went out. Darkness settled around her. Now was not the time to be thinking about feeling trapped. Vince was merely a heartbeat away.

It didn't matter.

The sensation of not being able to breathe, the cloying blanket of darkness, combined with a little flash-back of helplessness, triggered the beginnings of fear.

Somehow she couldn't completely escape feeling threatened. She put out a hand; she needed to push her way out of here, back to a well-lit room and the comfort of not feeling alone.

Instead of making her way out of the closet, she found herself in an even darker moment.

The wall she'd meant to push away from caved in, and she caved with it.

NINE

Vince was there in a heartbeat. He hauled her toward him, a little too easily, and then he secured her a bit too comfortably into his side. She wiggled a bit, then settled in as if she belonged plastered to his side.

"I thought the closet was a bit off in the way it was designed," Tamara muttered, trying to regain control.

Vince picked up the flashlight, shook it gently—it came back on—and pushed at the wall carefully. It gave some more, enough so Vince—once he let go of Tamara—could push it back.

Surprised, he said, "Wow, this old church is the last place I'd expect to find concealment construction."

"What's back there?"

After securing the false door, Vince answered, "There's a good-size safe with two boxes on top. Oh, and dust everywhere."

"Well," Tamara said, moving away from him, unnerved by how quickly his presence calmed her down, "as much as I'd like to haul everything out, we need to call the police."

"This stuff is covered with dust," Vince argued. "We're talking about decades of dust. It can't possibly have anything to do with what's going on downstairs or with you."

"Doesn't matter," Tamara said. "Right now everything is suspicious."

Tamara called the police, and in no time, the sheriff arrived. Jake peered in the closet, coughed at the dust and said, "Well, well, well."

Vince would have liked to hear a bit more deduction, but knew if he expressed a thought, he'd be escorted from the attic.

And he was curious.

The CSI guy returned and moved the boxes, photographed them and then focused on the safe.

Minutes ticked by. Minutes that had Vince itching to move, get involved, but not so Tamara. She managed to not only stand still, but to also stay quiet. It was impressive to watch her as she took in every movement in the room. She just didn't focus on the things—boxes and safe—but on the people. Vince would have missed the nuances, like how when the CSI technician pulled the latex gloves from his pocket, a few more pairs were evident.

"He's a perfectionist," Tamara whispered.

Then, there was how easily the man estimated the real perimeter of the closet without a tape measure.

"I knew that closet was off," Tamara whispered again.

"An average closet measures twenty-four by forty-eight. This closet's off in depth," Vince whispered back. "I'm impressed this guy didn't just double the width to get his estimate. I agree with him. The closet is probably only seventy in depth. Big enough for the safe."

"I'm dying to know what's in the safe," Tamara murmured. "Notice how Jake always stands slightly behind the man and to the left. They've worked together many times before. They're a team."

Alone, Vince would have been concentrating on how to get closer to the action. He'd be getting tools, breaking into the safe come drill bit or dynamite. Thanks to Tamara, he was seeing the details.

Finally, though, Vince couldn't stand it any longer. "Sheriff, it seems strange for a church to have concealment construction. I mean surely the Sunday morning collection is spent almost before it's counted."

Jake didn't even look at Vince when he answered. "You're probably right about that."

The CSI technician sounded almost relieved to hear contemplation. He took it as permission to talk. "Judging by the amount of dust, the safe's been hidden in that closet for decades."

"Can you open it?" Jake asked.

The technician got down on his hands and knees. He caressed the knob as if was made of gold.

"No, I'm not a safecracker. This is a three-combo lock. We'll need to call a locksmith at the least, but at the most, we'll be tempting fate with a soldering torch."

He stood, careful not to touch the safe, and backed into the room to sit on the floor in front of one of the boxes. Dust fluffed in the air, shimmering. Jake sneezed again.

In a way, Vince thought, the boxes looked like giant cigar boxes. The designs on the top had long faded. The main color was a mustard-yellow with swirls of brown. The CSI technician carefully slid a finger along the bottom edge of one.

He then tried to take off the lid.

It resisted.

Taking a knife from his pocket, the CSI technician

gently eased the edge of the lid away from the box until he could open it without damaging anything.

There was a vinyl deposit bag on top. Out came the CSI technician's notebook, and Vince watched while the man carefully recorded everything in the book. Underneath the bag were ledgers, all blank; receipt documents, again unused; and old reddish-colored paper tubes to roll coins in. At the bottom were old yellow pencils.

The CSI technician took a picture of the vinyl bag before he unzipped it. "Nothing." He opened his carry case, took out a bag, wrote something on it, and secured the zipper bag.

"Let's look at the other box," Jake suggested.

The CSI technician opened the second box. It was full of yellow, blue and green paper, trifolded, tightly wrapped in plastic. After a sketch, photos and a few minutes penciling something in his notebook, the CSI technician carefully lifted a corner and pulled one out. "Church bulletins."

"What year?" asked Jake.

The CSI technician read the front. "This one says Amhurst Church. 1962."

"Look at some of the others," Tamara ordered.

"'Amhurst Church, May 1962. Lesson today—Safe in the Arms of Jesus.' There's a brief description talking about never being alone. Here on the cover there's the church's address, the minister's name, guy by the name of Phillip Baker, and a list of elders and deacons."

He opened the bulletin. "Here we have a brief message from the minister. He's talking about this world not being your home. Hmm, he even mentions President Kennedy." The CSI technician looked up. "I think the theme of the day is keeping safe. Apparently, Kennedy had encouraged people to think about bomb shelters."

"You're kidding," Tamara said. "Kennedy did that?"

"Apparently." The CSI technician continued, "Here's a prayer request list. It's not very long. There's a few people who are sick, somebody is moving. The last one is for the Livingston family."

"Nineteen sixty-two?" Jake said. "The Livingston case? Boy, do I know that one. My grandmother said that family changed Grandpa's life."

Tamara watched, surprised, as Jake's facial features softened. "Go on," she said gently.

"My grandpa loved kids. Still does as a matter of fact. He's pretty much out of it, going senile, but whenever a school visits the care center, he perks up." Jake shook his head. "When I decided to go into law enforcement, my grandmother sat me down. I think she was hoping to change my mind."

"Why?" Vince said. "Your whole family was cops."

"Exactly."

Nobody said anything for a moment. It was the CSI technician who broke the silence. "And what about the Livingston case?"

"Give me a minute," Jake said. "It's been years since I thought about it. I wish I could remember names. All I recall is that the Livingston dad was mean. I guess he beat the kids, the wife. Grandpa was out there once or twice a week. I know that the kids got taken away and then given back. Something happened after they went back. I'm not sure. One of the kids got hurt. Grandpa blamed himself and the system. He went on a regular tangent."

"And because of that he coached baseball," Tamara said, "helped start a youth center—"

"—and the junior police academy," Jake finished.

The CSI technician put the bulletin aside and looked

through a couple more. "I don't see anything else about the Livingstons," he finally said. "But look, here's one that has a wedding announcement. Hey, it's your parents, Jake."

Jake, who was still behind the CSI technician and standing just to the left, bent down and peered at the announcement. "Sounds right. They were married in the early sixties, I think."

"Your dad attended church here?" Tamara asked. "Did your grandfather, too?"

"I'm sure he did. And he'd know all the goings-on," Jake agreed. "Problem is, right now he doesn't know what's going on, at all."

"Here's something else," the CSI technician said. "An announcement about ten-year-old Gloria Baker taking first place at a Bible Bowl."

"Gloria Baker," Vince said. "The nurse?"

Tamara pushed herself away from the wall and walked behind the CSI technician. "Does the bulletin list how many members the church had?"

The man looked and said, "It lists the attendance for the previous Sunday—forty-seven."

Tamara's smile was pure Cheshire. "Gloria Baker is probably the preacher's daughter or some sort of relative. This church wasn't that big."

Neither was Tamara's find.

The CSI technician determined the safe and the bulletins had nothing to do with the graffiti downstairs, and right after that he went back downstairs, Jake got a phone call and took off.

Tamara didn't even look disappointed. She just got out a notebook and started writing in it.

"What are you writing?" Vince asked.

"Questions to ask."

Vince was almost afraid to hear what came next.

Tamara smiled. "We need to pay a little visit to Gloria Baker."

It was a visit Vince had no intention of missing. Gloria versus Tamara just might be the show of the century.

Unfortunately, the show of the century had to wait. Gloria was working a double shift.

Vince called someone he knew and soon was carting the safe to his truck. "I'll get it open," he promised.

The CSI technician packed up and went home. Tamara went home right after that and did the unheard-of. She fell into bed and right to sleep. It wasn't even nine o'clock.

Tamara called Gloria the next morning, explained about finding the bulletins and wanting to ask questions about the old church.

"I'm busy all day, and tonight's church," Gloria said, "but you can come over after church."

How often had Lisa said the same thing… *You can come over after church.*

On her way to her building, Tamara called Vince and told him what Gloria had said.

"Church gets out pretty late," he said. "It's usually about eight."

"Let's not take a chance on her bailing on us," Tamara mused. "Let's surprise her and meet her at church."

Vince was quiet.

"It won't hurt you, you know."

"No," Vince finally admitted, "but I'll probably garner more attention than the minister."

He was right.

Tamara had called her sister to find out just exactly what happened on a Wednesday night at the Main Street Church. According to Lisa, it was laid-back. Laid-back was a concept Tamara wasn't comfortable with, exactly. She wore a pale blue two-piece with a teal shell jacket.

Vince, though went all out. He wore dark brown cords with a tan sweater. His brown shoes looked new and his hair was smoothed down.

"I like it sticking up," Tamara whispered in his ear.

"One more dig, and you're going to that church alone."

A handful of people were in the foyer. They were laughing and talking about the day's events. Nothing Tamara heard sounded as exciting as having one's tires flattened or finding a hidden safe.

All talk halted when she and Vince entered the area. Amy, Lisa's stepdaughter, was the first to break the silence. "Aunt Tamara. Mr. Vince." She skipped over, put her hand in Tamara's and whispered loud enough for all to hear, "Mommy's not feeling good. She's feeling fat."

It was the icebreaker they needed.

Miles came out of a side room, saw Vince and Tamara, and said, "About time."

After a moment, Tamara relaxed. Vince did, too.

A few minutes later, they were seated in the auditorium. It was only about a fourth full. "Wednesdays are more relaxed than Sundays. Less people attend so it's more intimate," Alex confided, as he checked his cell phone again. "I was tempted to stay home tonight, but Lisa insists she's fine at home by herself. Now I'm glad I came."

"Does Gloria Baker come on Wednesday nights?" Tamara asked.

Alex looked toward the front of the auditorium, right side. "I know where she'd be sitting and she's not there.

I do know sometimes she winds up working an extra hour or two if one of the other nurses runs late. Then, she might not make it. That's the only reason she'd miss church."

Miles delivered a sermon about some foolish rich man who lived a life without God. When his life was over, and he was in torment, he wanted to come back to Earth and warn others to not be like him.

God adamantly said no because the people the foolish man would tell would not listen.

Like the foolish rich man hadn't listened.

Almost too soon it was over.

Tamara'd never been to church before. As a child, she'd been invited. Both Lisa and Sheila had gone, occasionally. They'd enjoyed something called Vacation Bible School. But Tamara had considered it a waste of time. Who needed free Kool-Aid and cookies? It's not like the Kool-Aid and cookies tasted better just because they were served at a church instead of at home.

Now Lisa claimed they did taste better because of something called fellowship.

Tonight, as Angela, then Tali and Sharon, and finally Miles, all made sure to invite her to attend again, she had an inkling of what Lisa might have been talking about, an inkling that maybe she, Tamara, might need to listen.

"What did you think?" Tamara asked when they made it back to Vince's truck.

"I think it was okay. This once."

Tamara pulled out her cell phone and called Gloria's home. Gloria answered on the third ring. After a moment, Tamara hung up.

"She had something come up at the hospital and couldn't make it to church, but she said to come on over, she's home now."

They grabbed burgers and fries on their way. Tamara munched hers and watched as Vince effortlessly drove a truck with a clutch on the steering wheel while eating.

"How well do you know Gloria?" Tamara asked.

"I've run into her a time or two while working at the hospital."

"So, you don't know her outside of work?"

"Not at all."

Tamara tried to keep ketchup from dripping on her pants and said, "I wonder how many of the old Amhurst members now go to the Main Street Church? There was a whole cache of white-haired ladies sitting near the front. I'd love to talk to them."

"That means you plan on talking to them."

Tamara nodded. "Just think of all they can tell me. They remember this church when it was full of life, when it was functioning."

"I'm still amazed you're going to renovate it," Vince said.

Tamara smiled. "You know what it reminded me of, the first time I saw it?"

"No, what?"

"Remember the Christmas movie, with Jimmy Stewart and Donna Reed?"

Vince shook his head.

"It's called *It's a Wonderful Life*. There's an old fixer-upper in that movie, and Jimmy Stewart's character throws a rock at one of the windows. He thinks the place is beyond hope. Not so Donna Reed. She sees what the place could really be. That's how I felt when I saw the old Amhurst Church."

"I can understand that," Vince said.

Tamara believed him. He'd stood in the main room

and made suggestions she hadn't even imagined. What Vince couldn't see, didn't know, was restoring that old church was Tamara's way of telling the people who were throwing rocks at her that she was not letting them best her. No way, no how.

She'd just finished the last fry when Vince stopped in front of a small white house.

Two huge trees were in the front yard. A streetlight shone over the closed-in porch. Gloria lived in a residential neighborhood and across the street was a playground. Although it was after eight and on a weeknight, a group of teens lingered by a swing set.

Vince grunted.

"What's wrong?" Tamara asked.

"My brother's out there."

"So? It's not late and it seems like he's doing what most teenagers do." She looked closer. There were five kids—three boys and two girls. One kid was smoking, but she couldn't smell anything sweet so it probably was a cigarette.

It wasn't that hard to spot Vince's brother. He was taller than the rest, with lanky dark hair, and dressed all in black. He stood slightly away from the other four. The two girls were on the swings. One boy pushed both of them. The final boy was drinking something from a bottle.

Not smart.

At least it wasn't Vince's brother.

"That's Tommy Skinley," Vince said. "He's trouble."

"I've heard that said about you," Tamara remarked, hoping to ward off trouble.

"Which is why I recognize trouble. Stay here."

He left her at the truck, not that she stayed in, but she

circled around and leaned against the driver's-side door so she could see what he was doing.

She'd never gotten in trouble. She was too busy studying, but her middle sister Sheila had managed to anger their father more than once. A few times Tamara had sat in the passenger side while Dad pulled Sheila from places he thought she didn't belong.

Tamara never got out of the car. She'd been too afraid of her father. She'd also never defended Sheila, who truly hadn't been doing anything but what a typical teenager was prone to do.

Vince walked up to the swings. Both girls giggled. Tamara relaxed. Okay, the teens weren't scared of Vince. The boy who'd been pushing the swing stopped. In the stillness, Tamara could catch a word or two, enough to know that little brother wasn't happy about big brother showing up, and enough to know that Tommy Skinley wasn't pleased either.

After a moment, Vince's little brother stormed off. Then, so did the two girls and the swing pusher.

Tommy Skinley started to move, but Vince moved with him, taking the bottle from his hand and pouring what was left on the ground.

"They've been out here every night for the past week," came a voice from the other side of the truck.

Tamara moved to the hood and looked across at a small, blonde woman wearing a flowered T-shirt and jeans. "Are they causing any trouble?"

"More likely thinking up trouble," the woman replied.

"I think Vince is taking care of it." Tamara walked over and stood next to the woman. "Are you Gloria?"

The woman smiled. "Are you Tamara?"

"How'd you know?"

"Not long after you called this morning, Jake called. He wasn't a bit surprised that you wanted to talk to me."

"So, were you the preacher's kid or just a relative?" Tamara asked.

"The preacher's kid. Come on in. Looks as if Vince is going to take a few minutes."

"Oh."

Gloria was right. Vince had Tommy by the cuff of his shirt. The teenager struggled, but Vince clearly had it under control. Tamara took one step in their direction.

Gloria stopped her. "The sheriff was out here yesterday doing pretty much the same thing. Tommy needs to learn a lesson. He'll probably listen to Vince more than he will to Jake or his father. Listening to Vince will do him good."

As Tamara followed Gloria up the walk, she glanced back. Tommy had stopped struggling. He nodded a couple of times and then sagged against a jungle gym. Vince stayed where he was, talking, his hands moving a mile a minute.

There was a child-size bed on the porch; a big yellow dog slept on it. The dog raised his head, looked at Tamara and lay back down.

"Not much of a guard," Tamara remarked.

"I don't need a guard," Gloria responded. "God watches out for me."

Tamara bit back a response. She'd heard that statement more than once and hadn't really been impressed with the results. Bad things happened to good people. And she'd seen too many people with *no one* watching out for them.

Well, maybe it made Gloria feel good to think that God actually watched out for her here in little old Sherman, Nebraska.

He hadn't watched out for Tamara.

But then, she never asked him to.

The living room was decorated in different shades of blue and the theme was a mixture of antique country and religion. An old milk churner was in one corner. A display case held angel figurines and a few Bibles. There were family photos spread around the room, and lots of cross-stitched sayings on the walls.

"You do the cross-stitch?" Tamara asked, coming to a stop before one of the largest ones.

"While I watch television."

"Why doesn't this one have a scripture, like all the other ones?" Tamara studied a very detailed two-storied house, although *house* might be too tame a word. There was a sprawling lawn, columns, overhanging trees, arches and even a fountain. Underneath were the words, *My Mansion Will Not Fade With Time.*

"It's not from the Bible, exactly," Gloria said, "but the Word inspired it."

Tamara looked again, this time really focusing on the meaning of the words. The grass did need cutting. The columns had a few cracks. The trees drooped somewhat. The arches were in a place that did no good. The fountain didn't have any water flowing from it.

She'd missed that the first go-round.

Then, she thought about the words.

"It's my own design," Gloria said. "It came to me once, after a friend stopped by and made a comment about how little my house is. For a few days, I kept thinking about how little it was. I almost thought about moving. Then I realized that the size of my house truly didn't bother me. It's home."

Vince knocked. He looked annoyed as he came in,

but his expression brightened when Gloria offered coffee and homemade brownies. He headed for the couch and had to scoot the coffee table aside to find legroom. The couch groaned under his weight. He didn't even notice; he was too busy enjoying the brownies.

There was that saying about food and a man's stomach.

Tamara took a brownie and settled on the couch next to Vince.

He finished his brownie, then two, before he relaxed.

"I'm surprised Jake didn't stop us from coming over," Tamara began. "I'd think he'd want to question you first."

"You're the one in danger," Gloria said. She sat in a flowered armchair and picked up a hoop. She didn't start sewing right away, she just set it in her lap and leaned forward. "You're the one who purchased that old building. I'm amazed, I have to tell you. I didn't think Lydia would ever sell."

"You knew Lydia owned it?" Vince asked.

"Yes."

Vince sat up straight, surprise on his face. "How did you know?"

"Because her family owned most of Main Street. Nearly fifty years ago, it was her father who kicked the congregation out and shut the doors."

"Her family owned most of Main Street?" Tamara looked at Vince. "And do they still?"

He suddenly felt as if he was on the witness stand, and not as a well-prepared witness. A minute ago, he and Tamara had been on the same side. Now, with just a few words, she was on the offense.

He managed a halfhearted shrug, probably not the

response Tamara was looking for, but he'd made a promise to Lydia.

A promise he probably wouldn't keep for much longer. It was one thing for Tamara to ask questions, but quite another when the sheriff came along. When what he and Tamara had discovered up in the attic became public, what all Lydia had owned would most likely make the good people of Sherman gasp.

Tamara looked back at Gloria. "It was Lydia's father who evicted you. They owned the land the church was on. You're sure of this?"

"Very sure." Gloria pulled a needle from the fabric, and soon red thread was snaking in and out of the cloth. "I was the preacher's kid, an only child. A lot got said around the dinner table. Plus, I could hear my parents talking at night. Dad often thanked the Lord for Mr. Griffin's generosity. See, Dad had been preaching at a regular church on the other side of town. When it burned down, we didn't have the money to rebuild. Mr. Griffin heard about our plight and offered to let us use the farmhouse on Main Street. It was an interesting place to hold services. But after a while, and a few structural changes, it felt more like a church than a house. Dad kept thinking we'd buy it, but Mr. Griffin always said no. Dad was plenty surprised. Mr. Griffin was not a nice man. He had money and a beautiful family, but, according to my dad, money was his God."

"Money is important," Tamara said.

"And knowing what to do with it is even more important," Gloria shot back. "We had a beautiful building to meet in and really didn't pay rent or upkeep. The Griffins were a wealthy family. They did it all. Dad said Mr. Griffin was probably trying to earn marks toward Heaven. Not that you can get to Heaven that way."

"About when did your dad get evicted?" Tamara asked.

"1962."

"You can remember back that far?" Jake questioned.

"Certainly I remember. What I remember most is how devastated my father was." The hand clutching the embroidery hoop shook slightly. The other hand, the one with the needle, moved faster. "It was a great little church, growing, and a real asset to the community. My father preached one Sunday morning, everything was just fine, and that night he got a call from Lydia's father. Mr. Griffin wanted us out."

"And how long before the lease was up?" Tamara asked.

"There was no lease, not that I knew of. Dad and Mr. Griffin operated on a handshake. The Griffins were a strange family. Lorraine and her mother were regular churchgoers. Lorraine was the church secretary. She gave my dad no clue as to what was coming."

"Who was Lorraine?" Tamara asked.

"Lydia's sister. Lydia never came to church."

"I didn't know Lydia had a sister," Vince said.

"So, how long did they give you before you needed to vacate?" Tamara asked.

"Forty-eight hours."

Vince let out a whistle, and then said, "That's unfair. Surely—"

"Forty-eight hours or Mr. Griffin would contact his lawyer."

"And in forty-eight hours, you couldn't take everything. Is that why all the furniture and stuff got left behind?" Tamara questioned.

"When my dad showed up Monday morning, prepared to start packing, Mr. Griffin was waiting. He gave my dad a check to pay for all the furnishings, more than enough. Lorraine had boxes packed. She handed over most of the paperwork and such."

"You have a pretty good memory," Tamara said. "You were, what, nine when all this happened?"

"About." Gloria started plucking at an invisible thread on the canvas. "And it's not hard to remember something that changed your life. Dad pretty much had to start over. The elders rented space in a deserted store while they looked for land. People stopped attending services. I won't lie. Dad took it hard and we had a rough time of it."

"And you have no idea what caused the Griffins to suddenly want you out of the place?"

Gloria's hands stilled and she looked at Vince. "I have an idea, but it's not one you're going to like."

Vince raised one eyebrow. "Me?"

Gloria didn't say anything. Tamara knew the look of confliction. They were about to lose her. Sometimes, during a cross-examination, you wanted to take a witness to the breaking point. Then, if all went well, in anger or confusion they often said exactly what they were trying to hide.

"Vince," Tamara said, determined to get Lydia back into the story, "do you have any idea why Lydia's family would suddenly evict the church and then leave the building to deteriorate?"

Before Vince could answer, Gloria said, "Oh, it wasn't left to deteriorate. Not really. Someone from the Griffin family went in there every month to clean, make repairs and make sure nothing had been stolen. When Lydia's mom couldn't do it, Lydia moved back."

"There was really nothing to steal," Vince muttered. "And the only thing I know is that something happened, and it made Lydia incredibly sad. Sad enough that she left Sherman for a long time."

"Twenty-eight years," Gloria supplied.

Vince blinked. "How do you know that?"

"Because she came back when her mother died."

"And it was important enough for you to keep track of when she came back?" Tamara asked.

"No," Gloria said, "I didn't keep track. My mother did. We always did a family prayer right before bedtime. Until her death, my mother prayed for that family, and especially Lydia and little Billy, every single night."

"Why would she do that? Was Lydia in trouble? Is Lydia why you were evicted from the church?" The words tumbled out of Tamara's mouth so quickly she barely had time to put them in order.

Both Gloria and Vince looked at Tamara like she was nuts.

"Okay," she admitted. "I'm going a little fast, but I'm beginning to think that maybe I'm not a target, maybe the church is. And if we can find out why, maybe everyone will be better off. I mean, whatever secrets that church holds must be pretty serious. A prime piece of real estate stood empty for nearly fifty years."

"I've waited almost fifty years for someone to ask me these questions. No, wait a minute, I've waited almost fifty years to have someone who might actually take the information and do something with it. Now, Vince, I know how much you treasure Lydia, and she certainly has repented, but something happened forty-eight years ago, and whatever it was, it was swept under the carpet. After the church was evicted, Lorraine left town. Her father must have done something, been threatened, I don't know, but both Lydia and Lorraine left town, and Lorraine's never returned."

Tamara didn't say anything. She knew when to talk and when to keep quiet.

Vince, on the other hand, looked slightly shell-shocked. But then, he knew Lydia in a way Tamara didn't. And if Tamara wasn't mistaken, Lydia had been more or less a mentor for Vince.

"You think Lydia had something to do with the closing of the Amhurst Church?" he questioned. "That doesn't make any sense. She's a faithful member of the Main Street Church. She even got my mother to attend once. Now that's an accomplishment."

"She's a faithful member, *now.*"

"I don't see how Lydia figures into all of this," Vince argued. "You said Lorraine was the one who worked for the church, the one who packed everything up when Mr. Griffin didn't give your dad the forty-eight hours."

"Where is Lorraine now?" Tamara asked.

"That's just it," Gloria said. "No one knows."

"You'd think sisters would keep in touch," Tamara said. "My sisters act like I've upset Hallmark if there's not a steady stream of cards and visits."

Vince shook his head. "Not every family is like that. My family, for example—"

A loud popping noise interrupted his words. Gloria looked annoyed. "Not again," she murmured.

Tamara was already on the floor.

Gunshots.

TEN

Tamara started to get up. Vince pushed her back onto the floor and ordered, "Sit."

He crouched and quickly crawled to the window and peered out. "Nothing. I don't see anybody."

"Yet," Tamara muttered. She clutched her arms to her side and made herself breathe—in, out, in, out. "Was it a bullet?"

Gloria was surprisingly calm. "Being across from a park where teenagers hang out, you occasionally hear gunshots. That wasn't a bullet."

"I agree," Vince said. "I don't think it was a bullet. I think the popping noise was probably firecrackers. I'm not exactly sure what hit my truck."

"You're kidding. I didn't hear anything hit your car," Tamara said.

"You were too busy trying to run to the window and put yourself in danger." Vince moved from the window to the door and put his ear against it. "There's no one on the porch."

"The dog didn't bark," Tamara pointed out.

"The dog is fifteen years old and deaf." Gloria started to stand. Vince shot her a look that had her settling back in her seat.

"He only barks if I don't feed him fast enough," she finished.

"Ladies," Vince hissed. "Something funny is going on out there, and you're discussing the dog."

"True," Gloria said, standing up. "And we need to let Pepper in, in case there's a crazy teen out there."

"That could be it," Tamara said. For a moment, she almost felt giddy. "It's probably the kid you were talking to earlier."

"Tommy Skinley," Gloria supplied.

Vince stood and started for the door.

"No!" Tamara said, sounding a lot sharper than she intended. She lowered her voice. "What if it's not?"

Vince looked at the door and then back at Tamara. "I'll be fine. I'm sure it's the boys acting out. They're mad because—"

"Vince, let Pepper in," Gloria said.

Tamara started to get up, as did Gloria, but the look Vince shot them as he disappeared out the door kept both women in their seats.

A moment later the big, yellow lab was forced into the living room. When Pepper saw Gloria, he let out a low woof, gave Vince a dirty look and scooted over to sit at his master's feet. From behind Vince, Tamara could see the street and the headlights of a vehicle as it parked in front of the house.

"Sheriff made good time," Gloria stated. "One of the neighbors probably called."

Vince stood. "I'm heading outside, ladies. You stay here until we know the coast is clear." Before they could argue, he was out the door.

Gloria stood up first. She opened the front window

curtain, peeked out, and said, "It's worth the risk just to see a Frenci and a Ramsey work together."

"That bad, huh?" Tamara opened the curtain a bit more.

"It's not as bad as it used to be. I'm thinking that Vince's dad's taking off wasn't a bad thing. Debbie did the best she could raising her sons. Vince turned out just fine. Darren's coming around, and there's hope for little Jimmy."

"There's one more brother, right?"

"That would be Mickey. It's not my place, so if there's something you need to know about him, ask Vince. He'll tell you."

Vince and Jake stood by the police cruiser for a few moments, then walked over to Vince's truck. For a moment, Tamara thought she saw Vince smile as he looked at his newly broken back window. The sheriff seemed to think shaking his head the only necessary response.

"Think they'll figure it out tonight?" Gloria asked.

"Not a chance."

Gloria chuckled. "Well, let's leave them. Most likely you're right and it was one of the boys."

As if realizing that her audience wasn't convinced, Gloria put a reassuring hand on Tamara's shoulder. "We could put our heads in the sand and pretend this didn't happen, but it did, so let's go on. There's a few things I want to show you."

Tamara took a breath and followed Gloria into a back bedroom. While Gloria opened drawers, Tamara looked at the photographs and the cross-stitching on the walls.

For a small-town nurse and preacher's daughter who had never married, Gloria'd had quite a life. The bedroom walls told a story of travel—France, Africa, England and more. There were pictures of friends.

Tamara recognized, most of them from her little sister's church.

If I'm single all my life, what would my photographs say about me?

Tamara had a few family photos. And, she'd had her picture in the paper more than once while working on a case. And then there were the newspaper photos during the stalking.

She was a distinct blur in all of them because the press knew better than to feature a victim.

Breathe in; breathe out.

So far, the photos of Tamara's life would depict a little bit family, a little more work and a whole lot of fear.

"I keep these in an album," Gloria said. "They were my father's favorite. It's the church, back in its glory days."

The outside of Tamara's building was a gleaming white, not peeling and faded like today. The lawn was much the same, except there used to be a sign announcing Amhurst Church, complete with the minister's name, meeting times and such. The weathervane from atop the building wasn't leaning. Gloria even had pictures from inside.

"Oh, can I borrow these?" Tamara sat on the bed and took the album in her lap. She turned pages, seeing what the classrooms and the gathering room had looked like, the kitchen and, finally, the minister's office up in the attic.

"My dad loved his office. He said sermons were never the same when he couldn't look out the window at Main Street."

"Jake's still outside," Vince said from the doorway. "He'll be in in a minute."

"Go ahead and come in, Vince," Gloria urged. "It's just a bedroom."

Vince didn't appear convinced, but then, his head almost touched the top of the door frame.

"Gloria's showing me pictures of what the church looked like when her father was the minister there. See." Tamara held up the album. "Here's the office. I am so impressed."

Vince didn't come sit on the bed. With Tamara and Gloria already sitting there, there wasn't room.

"A typical minister's office," Gloria said.

Vince took the album from Tamara's hand and studied it. "Your father was a collector," he finally said.

"Yes, Daddy was fascinated with history, especially if it had to do with the church."

Vince put the album in Gloria's lap and pointed to two items—a cross and a Bible.

"Where are these items now?"

"Some went missing before Daddy was evicted. He always wondered if Mr. Griffin knew their worth. Then, forty-eight hours just wasn't enough time for Daddy to get everything. He waited a few weeks before approaching Mr. Griffin about letting him get the rest of his personal belongings. By the time Dad got back inside the church, somebody had taken just about everything important."

Vince's expression turned granite.

"What's wrong?" Tamara asked gently.

"That cross is in a box in my uncle Drew's shed waiting to be carted off to the Goodwill. And that Bible went home with Reverend Pynchon a few weeks ago. No wonder he looked as if he struck gold. My uncle's worried about a whole lot more than protecting Lydia. Somehow, he's trying to protect himself."

* * *

Someone banged on the front door. "That'd be the sheriff," Gloria said, heading out of the bedroom.

Tamara stayed on the bed; Vince continued to stare at the album.

"It's all connected," she said softly. "This all has to do with the church. It's not really somebody after me."

The relief on her face almost moved Vince to sit on the bed beside her. Instead, he stood there, helpless, trying to force himself to remember he was working *for her.* Unfortunately, he kept finding himself working beside her, really working *with her.*

And not because he was getting paid, but because way too quickly she'd filled a hole in his life.

A hole he'd dug on purpose.

One best left empty.

He cleared his throat and said, "I think you're right. We need to talk with Lydia. I don't think she'd have sold the church. Billy did it without her knowing it. His selling certainly hit a hot button with my uncle. And somebody's working with him."

"Any idea who?"

For some reason, the question angered him. For years, people had turned to him when his brothers got into trouble. He'd always managed to laugh it off. This time it was Tamara asking, and she should know better.

"If I had an idea, I'd have told both you and the sheriff. As far as I know, Drew has no friends. Maybe he had cronies during his youth, but they're either dead or near it."

"What if Drew isn't the only one who wants to keep the old place empty? What if somebody else is trying to scare me away?" Tamara asked.

"What do you mean? You mean in addition to Drew?"

"That's exactly what I mean. We know there's a reason why Lydia didn't sell the old church, but she's not a suspect. Unless things have really changed over at Sherman Oaks Nursing Home. We know that Drew wants to help Lydia out, enough to try to burn the church down. How that's helping her, I'm not sure. We also know that there's at least one other person out there trying to scare me away. Who else could be keeping secrets?"

"Everybody has secrets," Vince said.

"If Drew's involved," Vince said finally, "one secret's enough."

"If I sell the building, maybe Sherman will become a safe little town again."

"And maybe when we get the safe open, the secret will be exposed, and you won't have to sell."

Tamara nodded.

"And you'll stick around."

He hadn't meant to say the words aloud. Luckily, Tamara was too busy thinking about her problems to recognize what Vince had almost let slip. He handed her the photo album. "We'll figure this out. In a few months, we'll laugh, and all the neighbors will compliment you for bringing the old building back to its original beauty."

She didn't look convinced.

"Tomorrow, first thing," Vince said, "I'm going to take care of the safe, and then I'll go talk to Drew. Find out about the cell phone. Find out how he got those items that belonged to Gloria's father. He probably stole them all those years ago. But, you know, I can't imagine him trying to burn the church over that. I mean, nobody missed those items. There's gotta be something else he's trying to hide."

"I should have asked sooner," Tamara said. "How is he?"

"In a lot of pain. Second-degree burns over both hands and most of his right arm. He also has burns on his knees and legs. They have him pretty heavily sedated. I'll have to get to him at just the right time."

"Tamara! Vince!" Gloria called.

Clutching the album, Tamara followed Vince into the living room.

"You want to file a complaint?" Jake said to Vince. He'd already taken a seat in the flowered armchair.

"No. There's really no lasting damage. Darren can fix the back window. The rest is just broken glass."

"Gloria tells me your brother and some of his friends were in the park earlier tonight. You think they were up to any other pranks, besides targeting you?"

"They were just hanging out. I got on their bad side by asking a few questions."

"About what?" Jake asked.

"Drinking and skipping school."

Jake didn't look surprised. He took a small notebook from his pocket and wrote something.

Gloria looked from her front window, to Vince, then Jake and obviously decided it was a good time to change topics. "So, Tamara, Jake said you'd stumbled on a few things, but I thought maybe papers or something. That secret compartment's perfect for a lawyer's office. My dad loved all the extras that old building had."

"Do you know all the extras?" Tamara asked.

"No. I just know what my dad was willing to share."

"Now might be a good time for you to share," the sheriff said. He still had his notebook out.

"Lydia, of course, could tell you more. Her family practically settled the town," Gloria replied. "Anyway, Lydia's great-grandfather Jacob Griffin built the house in the early nineteen-hundreds. It started life as a farm. The parking lot used to be a cow pasture. Dad had pictures somewhere. Me, I wouldn't want the cows quite that close."

Vince almost laughed at the expression on Tamara's face. She'd probably want the cow pasture put in the next town.

"It's hard for me to imagine a farmhouse turning into a church," Tamara admitted.

"Well, you have to remember this was decades ago, and we were a small congregation. My dad was just thrilled that we didn't have to rent an empty store. At one time," Gloria continued, "way before we moved in, there was a barn out back. Then as the town grew, there came more streets, more people, and the farm became just a house. Even the barn became a house. It burned down, and a bigger, better house appeared. I guess Lydia's uncle lived in what's now the church while Lydia and her family lived where the barn used to be. Lydia's uncle never married and apparently was quite a character. People say he walked around town as if he was on military patrol. Daddy had pictures of him, too."

"How did it get the name Amhurst Church?" Tamara asked.

"When Lydia's uncle died, the place sat empty for a few years. Lydia's dad rented it to the church in the late fifties. At that time, Amhurst was the name of the street.

Sherman grew. It merged with another small town, and two streets became one. Amhurst became Main Street and soon no one remembered Amhurst."

"Are there any other hidey-holes?" Vince asked.

"There's a space the size of a shoe box somewhere near the baptistery."

"Can you show it to me?" Tamara asked.

"I'm pretty sure."

"I want to be there. Could there be others?" Jake asked.

Gloria nodded. "I'm sure there are. I just don't know where they might be."

"You were talking about Lorraine earlier?" Tamara said. "You said she packed up your dad's stuff and it was waiting the day after you were kicked out of the church. Could she have put the stuff in the secret compartment?"

"She probably knew about the compartment. She did the bulletin, typed up the sermon notes, did the accounting. Dad said he'd never had a secretary so capable."

"Capable of emptying out the safe, too?" Tamara said.

Both Jake and Vince nodded.

Gloria shook her head. "Not a chance. Lorraine wouldn't have done that. Dad said she was practically crying when she handed everything over. Whatever had her dad in a snit had her all upset. She took off a couple of days later, I'm not sure how many, and she's not been back."

"Lydia ever talk about her?" Tamara asked Vince.

"I didn't even know Lydia had a sister," he said.

"Twins. They were twins."

Gloria looked at Tamara. "If you're that curious, you can ask some of the ladies who go to the Thursday morning Bible class. You saw a few of them at church last night. There are a few who were Lydia and Lorraine's contemporaries."

"How well do you know Lydia?" Jake asked.

"Not well," Gloria admitted. "I work when they have Ladies' Bible Study, and during regular services she sits on the other side. Maybe I'm holding a grudge against the Griffin family. If that's the case, I need to let it go. But, in all fairness, I don't know Lydia because back then, when my dad was preaching, she didn't really attend church much. Or at least not that I remember. She was a wild one. I can remember many a prayer my dad uttered over her."

"Lydia?" Vince said. "Our Lydia? She was a wild one?"

"Those sisters were as different as night and day."

"What changed Lydia?" Tamara asked.

"Probably having Billy," Jake said.

"No." Gloria again was shaking her head. "I can remember Dad praying about Billy, about the atmosphere he was growing up in. Lydia didn't change until she was much older."

"I remember my parents talking about that, too," Jake added, suddenly looking antsy. "Something about her and my grandpa Jasper. They said he used to watch out for her. I could never imagine why. Of course, sounds like she rehabilitated."

"Some people do change when they get older," Gloria said.

"Except for Uncle Drew," Vince muttered.

No one contradicted him.

"What happened when Lorraine went missing?" Tamara asked. "I mean, what did her parents say? Did they report her missing?"

"She's not a cold case on my desk," Jake answered.

"Her parents," Gloria said, "up until they died, claimed that she eloped and that they were hearing from her regularly, getting letters and such. They even had pictures of both Lydia and Lorraine as they aged."

"You see these pictures?" Tamara asked Vince.

"The few times I was in Lydia's house there were only pictures of her and Billy."

"If she eloped, why wouldn't she come back to visit her parents after she and her new husband had time to settle down?" Tamara wondered. "I mean, lots of people eloped during the sixties."

"Or they ran off and didn't bother to get married. The era of free love was beginning."

"And that wouldn't have gone over well with the parents," Vince said, looking at the sheriff, who was suddenly looking at his watch again.

"When and why did Lydia move?" Tamara asked next.

"Come to think of it, she left a few weeks after Lorraine," Gloria said, then gasped.

"What's wrong?" Tamara asked, starting to get up.

"Oh, my, sometimes there's something you haven't thought of in years, and when you finally do remember, it all makes so much sense."

"Care to share?" the sheriff asked.

"I remember briefly thinking there was something funny about your uncle Drew the other day, claiming he needed to take care of Lydia. Something I should remember. I just remembered why I thought it was funny."

She had everyone's attention.

"Fifty years goes by and things that were once the makings of gossip and speculation get lost."

"Spill it," Jake said sardonically.

"Well," said Gloria, "I'm thinking there's not too

many people alive that either care or care to remember who Billy Griffin's father is."

"Gloria," Jake warned, "Just spill it." He held his tiny notebook in a death grip. Tamara recognized the stance. Back when she was a practicing lawyer, sometimes she'd mangled whatever she held in her hand during a particularly intense briefing.

Gloria looked at Vince. "If I remember right, Drew is Billy's father."

ELEVEN

Tamara had only been a practicing lawyer for two years, but in those two years, she'd been working with the best. And the best advised, *Be surprised at nothing*.

Vince's mouth hung open in silent awe. Tamara put her hand on his knee. He didn't move, not even a little.

Even more surprising was the sheriff.

It looked to Tamara like Jake was about to come out of his seat. The sheriff's hands were shaking as they wrote in the tiny notebook he carried. He bit down on his lip, and Tamara figured if she didn't say anything, pretty soon they'd need to hand him a tissue to wipe away the blood.

She'd also learned, *Attack while surprise is still on your side*. "Why does this surprise you, Jake?" Tamara asked gently.

He looked up. "Oh, it doesn't. I'm—"

He stuttered to a halt. Everyone was looking at him. Gloria, with concern. Vince, still with no expression. Tamara leaned forward.

Jake cleared his throat. "Seems like the time for secrets to come out. I'm surprised, that's all. And I wish my father were still alive. All these years, because

Grandpa had such a soft spot for Lydia, we, the whole family, thought Billy was his."

Now it was Gloria's turn to look surprised. "Oh, no," she said softly, "Not a chance."

"Once again," Vince said drily, "my uncle Drew will be making headlines."

"He was in this morning's paper," Gloria agreed. "About the fire."

Vince filled Jake in on the items Drew might have stolen. Just as the clock chimed eleven, Gloria said, "I don't know about the rest of you, but I get up with the chickens."

Vince's hand was pressed against Tamara's back as he held open the door and guided her out to the porch. Behind her, she could hear muted words. She ducked under Vince's arm and looked back into the living room.

Gloria and Jake were huddled in the middle of the room. Gloria's hand, like Vince's, was gently pressed against Jake's back. Both their heads were bowed. The only words that Tamara could hear from the muted prayer were "Help me, Father."

Tamara didn't even look at the clock when she got home. If it struck midnight, she didn't care. She shed her clothes, didn't bother with a shower, and fell into bed whispering the words, "Help me, Father."

Exhausted, she slept and even the dreams and the storm clouds gathering outside couldn't interrupt her sleep.

If there was one thing a lawyer knew how to find, it was a birth certificate. Tamara held it in her hand the next morning. William Robert Griffin had been born to Lydia Irene Griffin in 1959. The father's name was Drew Randolf Frenci. There was no marriage certificate on file.

Tamara hurried down the city courthouse walkway to her car. Gray and black clouds low in the sky moved with her. Shivering, she pulled out her cell phone. Vince always answered right away. She'd already figured out he thrived on interruptions. He was her first call. At the moment she didn't have a next call unless she wanted to talk to the sheriff.

The line started to dial just as the first raindrops fell. One landed on the back of Tamara's hand. Another right on the open cell phone. Tamara stopped, wiping away the moisture on her phone. Her hand stilled as she cleared away the rain. Vince Frenci's name was on her cell phone. If she looked at the "calls dialed" section of her cell phone, almost every call was to Vince.

He answered before she had time to angst about how often she'd been calling him. First came static, then finally, the sound of a hammer drill in the background.

"Drew's a daddy," Tamara announced, instead of saying hello. "If we doubt the birth certificate, or if we doubt Gloria's memory, we can always fall back on DNA."

There was a slight pause. Vince yelled something and the noise diminished. Then, he said, "I've only met Billy once and he doesn't look like Drew."

"Good thing, because Drew's a bit scary-looking, but unfortunately, it means nothing. Look at Lisa and me. She's all girly perfection, and I'm…" Tamara stopped. Almost afraid of what she'd been about to say, about to admit.

It was time to start calling her sister Lisa more often, not just to check on Lisa's condition but to assure Lisa that Tamara was all right. Plus, maybe it was time for Tamara to start talking about Vince, all he was doing, the way he was making Tamara feel.

"If you're not all girly perfection, then what are you?" he asked.

Poor man. He hadn't a clue the corner he could back himself into.

No way did Tamara want to start the comparison of sisters. Lisa had always been the beautiful one. She walked into a room and the guys started migrating her way as if magnetized. Sheila was just as bad. She wasn't as girly girl as Lisa, but she was fun. Usually, growing up, when someone knocked on their door, they wanted Sheila. She knew what was going on, when and where.

Lisa did, too, but she usually seemed to drift to the right places.

Tamara didn't know the hot spots and she never drifted. Every move she made was carefully planned. As a teenager, she'd much preferred staying home with a good book. As a college student, she'd found many people with a like mind, and she'd studied and done all the things to make her résumé look good. As a lawyer, back in Phoenix, she'd been in her element. Then, too, she'd been a year away from marrying someone very much like her.

William Massey had done more than mess up her life. He'd changed her way of thinking, changed what she cared about and why.

Tamara hadn't thought romantically about Terry Burnes in weeks. Considering how recent their breakup was, that made no sense. She should be missing him! Thinking about him!

Instead, it was Vince she thought about in the morning, and Vince she thought about during the day. And Vince she said good-night to.

It was Vince who got most of her cell phone time as well.

Maybe when it came to the type of men she was attracted to, it was a good change. Because Vince listened to her even when it wasn't about work.

Hmm.

"Are you still there?" Vince asked.

"I'm here, and it's nothing. I'm just feeling the repercussions of the past few days."

Someone shouted and Vince shouted back a response.

"I can tell you're busy," she said. "Call me after you talk with Drew."

"Wait," Vince said quickly. "I was going to call you during break. I took the safe to the shop this morning. They called ten minutes ago. It's empty."

Tamara almost wanted to chuckle. Answers never came easy. An empty safe was like an empty Christmas stocking.

After ending the call, Tamara dialed Lisa's number. Her sister was due to give birth in two days.

No one answered.

Taking a breath, Tamara dropped her phone into her purse, headed for her car and drove to the old church. Surely, based on how much time the police had spent at the building, no one would try anything today.

The CSI technician was gone. He'd scooted pews away from the walls and now they were all jumbled to one side. The floor where he'd been working was miraculously clean, but the floor where Tamara stood and everywhere else was pure dust except for footprints. The front of the church was untouched. The baptistery was an empty shell; the communion table and pulpit looked lonely.

The only thing that didn't fit the spiritually somber mood was the graffiti. Too bad the CSI technician hadn't painted over it.

Tamara walked through the room and headed for her favorite place—the attic.

She set her purse on top of the mahogany desk, turned on the portable CD player she'd brought with her, and then sat cross-legged in front of the boxes of old bulletins. How funny that the old mimeograph machine was still in the office. Tamara wondered if it still worked. Too bad an old typewriter hadn't been left. It would add to the retro feel Tamara suddenly wanted for her office.

The Church bulletins were full of names Tamara didn't know. People were moving out of town, moving in, wanting prayers. The Livingstons were mentioned often. Unfortunately, exactly why they needed prayers was not mentioned. The Amhurst Church took care of the poor. They did door knockings and car washes. The youth met every week.

Lorraine Griffin's name was mentioned in almost every bulletin and not because she happened to be the secretary. She organized a singles' movie night. She helped with a baby shower. She taught a third-grade Bible class.

Tamara thought back to the photos in Gloria Baker's house, the photos that told of a fulfilling life. Gloria had said Lorraine had just graduated from college around the time she left town. Her legacy wasn't in photos but in deeds.

Lydia was mentioned in almost every bulletin, too. Hmm, Lydia had run away from home. Lydia had agreed to see a counselor. Lydia was hanging with the wrong crowd. The Griffin family wanted prayers on her behalf.

The prayers must have worked for Lydia to become the role model Vince kept talking about.

Tamara reached the bottom of the box just as her cell phone rang. She didn't recognize the number, so it wasn't Vince.

"I've just called the sheriff," Gloria Baker said. "I came home from work for my lunch hour and there was red stuff on my door. When I got close enough, I could see that somebody had painted the words *Stop Talking or You're Next.*"

"Take it seriously," Tamara advised.

"Oh, I am," Gloria said. "Very seriously. I know all about what's going on with you, and I'm terrified. See, they misspelled the word *you're* on my door, too."

As Vince watched his uncle sleep, he tried to find a comfortable position in the only chair Drew's hospital room provided.

It was not designed for a big man.

Then, too, Vince wasn't used to sitting still with nothing to do. *Okay, old man,* Vince thought. *Just exactly what am I going to ask you when you wake up? Shall I start with, are you Billy's father? Or maybe, why did you try to burn down Tamara's church?*

Yeah, definitely, Tamara's church was more important.

Because Tamara was more important.

Vince pulled out his cell phone. No messages; no surprise. He'd had the thing on all morning, waiting to hear from Tamara.

His boss, John Konrad, had called four times. Each time it was a question of *how many shall I order or what time will you be done?* His mother had called once, more than a little angry. She rambled on about how hard it was to manage a teenager when she worked nights. Apparently, Jimmy had joined the ranks of his brothers. No, he hadn't stolen a car, but he'd been driving Tommy's car and had hit a parked car. Instead of stopping, he and Tommy had driven off, leaving the scene of an accident complete with two witnesses.

She also grumbled about Jimmy's performance in school. And then, she asked if he knew where Jimmy was. Before Tamara, Vince had kept better track of his little brother. Time to reevaluate. Leaving Tamara out of the equation made lots of sense. His family's disorder would offend her sense of order.

Darren, Vince's oldest brother, wasn't much help. Darren believed in taking care of himself and only himself. Vince wanted to do that. The difference between Vince and Darren was Vince always answered his cell phone.

Mickey was still serving time. He wouldn't be eligible for parole for five years.

Most times, Vince could push thoughts of his family far away. Not right now. Because of Tamara, Vince was ready to take Drew on. Because of Tamara, he was thinking about the dynamics of family, and if having a family was worth it.

Drew mumbled.

Now, Drew was a true loner. Or at least he'd been a true loner for all of Vince's life.

If Vince had the brains of a gnat, he'd be running. Far, far away from Tamara Jacoby and her red hair and green eyes.

He'd noticed them last year, at Alex and Lisa's wedding. Back then, he'd had to walk down the aisle with her. This was where he'd personally experienced her gift for organization as well as her missed military calling.

Since he had a gift with a hammer, she'd made him her right-hand man. He wasn't sure she even asked, more like ordered. If not for Alex and the bride-to-be, Lisa, he might have been annoyed. Instead, he'd pitched in willingly and by the end of the wedding, he'd been a little impressed and a lot attracted.

Like a bug to a light.

She was one light he definitely needed to keep turned off. Back then, he hadn't really worried. She'd been engaged, and she lived in a different state.

Lawyers and construction workers didn't necessarily run in the same circles. Half the time, even when not working, she wore a dark blue three-piece suit, with sensible black heels, and carried a no-nonsense purse. If not for that glorious hair, she'd almost pull off the persona of no-touch woman.

But he'd seen her vulnerable. He'd seen her standing stock-still in front of the old Amhurst Church, afraid to move.

She'd bounced back.

"Erump." Drew might have spoken a word, or maybe he was simply moaning.

Vince looked at the time again. Only five minutes had passed. No way could he stick around much longer. His lunch hour was only thirty minutes long.

In the small town of Sherman, Vince could count on one hand the people who mattered to him. Lydia Griffin had been on that list since childhood. That she'd been involved with his uncle made no sense.

Vince admired Lydia. She'd taught him hard work, physical work, how to work with the land. She, up until the past six months, had worked with a kind of silent precision he admired, especially for someone in her late seventies. She was just a few years younger than Drew, but in personalities, they were aeons apart.

Lydia didn't mind riding a lawn mower or getting her hands in the dirt. She said it was fun. Vince figured that people in their seventies had a different idea of fun than people in their twenties.

"Would you like some company?" said Miles Pynchon, standing in the doorway. "Gloria said you were in here. How's he doing?"

Vince studied Drew. If anything, his uncle had stilled somewhat. Maybe the presence of a man of God had that effect.

"He's heavily medicated."

Miles came all the way into the room and stood by the bed. Unlike Vince, he looked at home in a hospital room. He took Drew's hand gently. He didn't seem to notice the gnarled fingers or bulging veins. Miles's fingers tightened. He looked at Vince. "I'm going to say a prayer. Would you like me to do it out loud or silently?"

"Silently," Vince answered automatically.

Miles bowed his head. His lips moved and at first he didn't pray, but recited, "…it was not with perishable things such as silver or gold that you were redeemed from the empty way of life handed down to you from your forefathers…" Then, he bowed his head all the way in prayer. He looked at peace.

Vince suddenly doubted his choice. What would having the prayer said aloud hurt? Could a simple prayer really offer peace?

Then Vince noticed what Miles had clutched under his arm. Not one Bible but two. The man probably knew he'd need reinforcements when it came to dealing with Drew.

"Amen." Miles ended the prayer and walked over to stand near Drew's hospital bed. "Jake visited the church this morning. He had some interesting questions. Of course, my family is not originally from here, so we don't remember when Gloria Baker's father was the minister."

"So, you couldn't help him?"

"Not with his questions about Reverend Baker, personally, but I did have something to share about Drew." Miles set a slender Bible on the hospital bed. "This is the Bible I carry when I'm doing my rounds. I have one in my office with ripped pages, all my notes and such. I also have a Bible at home that's my personal one. I can certainly understand Reverend Baker's attachment to old Bibles and such."

He took the other Bible from under his arm. Now Vince noticed that it was encased in a plastic bag.

"This is the one I found at Drew's place when I was helping you all those weeks ago. I knew when I left that it was a treasure. I just found out yesterday morning how much a treasure."

With all that had happened at Gloria's the other night, the Bible artifacts had been left out. Vince took the Bible and examined the book through the plastic. "Okay, what's so special about this Bible to make it such a treasure?"

"It's a 1621 King James Bible. I carefully went through it—scared to death, by the way, that I might damage it—and none of the pages are missing. Except for the cover, it's in great condition. I called a friend of mine at a Bible college. He's an expert on rare books. He wants to see it, but conservatively, over the phone, he said the book could fetch as much as six thousand dollars."

"Six thousand dollars!"

Miles nodded. "And here's what I need to tell you. I only made a dent in that shed and carried away this Bible and a cross. Vince, there are still other boxes packed away in there."

"So, some of the trash Drew hoarded could indeed be worth a fortune?"

"Exactly."

"So the silver and gold you were just talking about has to do with what's in the shed?"

Miles nodded. "It's from a scripture. Never really made much sense to me until I applied it to what I found and to Drew. It's in the first book of Peter. You might want to read the Bible. It can help. Silver, gold, antique Bibles, they're all worthless when compared to the Word. Your uncle may have a cache in his shed, but he has emptiness in his heart."

"Erump," Drew muttered.

Vince quickly looked at his uncle. Miles moved to his side. Drew's eyes didn't open, but he was no longer twitching.

Miles stayed by Drew's side. Nothing changed. "Maybe we need to take the conversation somewhere else?" Miles suggested.

"Like back to my uncle's yard and all that mess," Vince agreed.

"Drew's yard sounds like a pretty good place," came a voice from the doorway. Jake Ramsey leaned against the door frame. Tamara stood next to him.

Drew's eyes snapped opened.

A monitor beeped and before anyone had time to move, a nurse hustled into Drew's room and effectively hustled everyone else from the room. They moved down to the cafeteria. Tamara wanted to walk with Vince, but he walked the whole way with his phone to his ear. He hung back as the rest of them went through the food line before sitting.

"Drew didn't utter a word, but his look spoke volumes," Miles handed the old Bible over to Jake. "I'm assuming you heard everything?"

"I heard enough," Jake answered.

Tamara quietly nibbled on a sandwich and watched Vince. It was obvious he was talking to his mother. Something was bothering him and it didn't have anything to do with old Bibles. Tamara watched as he started talking, stopped, listened, talked again and shook his head.

Finally, Vince took his seat. He looked distracted but still determined. He was the only one not bothering with food.

Jake took out his notebook. "I'll talk with Drew's doctor. See when Drew will be strong enough, alert enough, to talk. Afterward, I'll also get together with Gloria and see what she has to say about the missing items. Then, Vince, let's head out to your uncle's place and see what else we can find."

Vince nodded.

"Poor Gloria." Jake shook his head. "She's had more excitement the past two days than she has the past two decades."

"I wouldn't call her poor when she's about to get her daddy's stuff back," Vince said.

"She puts on a good front, all professional and stern, but she was scared this morning, really scared."

"This morning?" Vince asked. "Don't you mean last night?"

Tamara raised an eyebrow and looked at Vince. "You don't know?"

"Don't know what?"

Tamara quickly filled him in on the warning on Gloria's door.

Vince looked at Jake. "You know, sometimes the truth stares you in the face and you're just too dumb or maybe too blind to see it."

"I—"

Vince raised his hand. "No, I'm not talking about you, really, I'm talking about me. I've spoken to my mother twice today. My little brother Jimmy skipped school today. She's been having some trouble with him, has been for a while, but I didn't put two and two together until just now."

"I wish you'd share with the rest of us," Tamara urged.

"Red paint on the doors," Vince said simply. He looked at Miles. "Remember, we started cleaning Drew's yard. We barely made a dent, but he had plenty of paint cans back there. I'll bet when we get that search warrant, we'll find paint the exact shade as what got painted on both Tamara's and Gloria's doors, as well as Gloria's father's stolen property."

"They're just kids," Tamara protested. She could see the hurt on Vince's face. The worry.

"Then, yesterday, they were in the park and had the guts, or stupidity, to set off firecrackers and throw a glass bottle at my car."

"That might not have been your brother. Maybe it was just Tommy Skinley, acting alone," Tamara mused, looking at Jake and hoping for a slight nod, anything. "Gloria said it was probably Tommy."

"Oh, I'm sure Tommy Skinley is involved," Vince said slowly.

The sheriff nodded but didn't say a word.

"Then, today," Vince continued, "my brother skips school and the school calls and—"

Before he could continue, his cell phone, as if cued,

rang. It only took him a moment to get to, "Yeah, Mom, did you find it?" Then, he listened carefully, looked up at the sheriff, and said, "555-7265?"

Jake didn't need prompting. He took out his notebook, flipped back a few pages and nodded. "That's the number."

Vince hung up. "Jimmy has Drew's cell phone. He just might be the accomplice."

TWELVE

Vince looked at Tamara. "The guys I work with have been joking around a lot lately, telling me I was pretty smart to get involved with a lawyer, me being a Frenci and all. I guess they were right. If my little brother is involved, I'm going to have to beg you for leniency."

"He into Japanese symbols?" the sheriff asked.

"Tommy Skinley is," the minister piped up. "His parents showed me some of his drawings. They seem to think he'll be a graphic artist when he's older."

"It's worth investigating." Jake took the last bite of his sandwich, carefully tucked the old Bible under his arm, and gathered all his trash. "Oh, by the way, I looked the Livingston case up. No wonder my grandfather became such an advocate for kids. There were three kids, all under ten. My grandfather must have logged a visit a week to the place. Whatever was going on kept falling under the heading of neglect instead of abuse. Until 1962. Then, while the children's father was drunk, he pushed the three-year-old down the stairs. Claimed it was an accident."

Tamara gasped. She heard stories like that all the time. It never got easier.

"The little boy didn't die," Jake said. "But the dad let

him lie on the basement floor until the mother got home. Kid had two broken legs and a concussion. It made the paper, and my grandfather got a reprimand for some of the cutting remarks he made about a system that returns children to abusive parents."

"What happened after that?" Vince asked.

"After that, my grandfather started working with kids. As for the little boy, I don't know. The family moved. No wonder Grandpa changed," Jake said, leaving.

"If something goes down with either Jimmy or Tommy, call me," Miles said to Vince, watching the sheriff march out the door. "Your mom's been taking care of things alone for too long. God can help."

Tamara was proud of Vince. He didn't even blink. He actually seemed to be listening and maybe even inclined to do what the preacher asked.

"Tommy and his folks have been attending Main Street since Tommy was a baby," Miles continued.

"Didn't help him stick to the straight and narrow," Tamara said. She'd heard too many parents insist that their son or daughter couldn't possibly be to blame. After all, they'd taken their child to church.

"Ah," said Miles, "but you forget. Only one perfect man walked the Earth. He's neither at this table nor in this town."

Vince scooted his chair back. "I need to let my boss know I'm taking the rest of the day off, and then I've got to find Jimmy."

"I'll come with you," Tamara offered.

"No, this is family stuff. I'd better do it alone."

Before Tamara could say anything else, Vince had his cell phone out and was making another call. He walked to the door slowly, shoulders weighed down.

Miles laid a hand on Tamara's shoulder. "I'll do what I can, make a few phone calls, maybe drive around a bit, see if anyone has spotted either Tommy or Jimmy."

"I guess, then, I'll go to the church and finish cleaning out the attic."

Miles stood. "I've got a few more people to see here at the hospital. You have my cell phone number?"

When she shook her head, he handed her his card. Tamara stuck it in her purse and started to head for the exit. But Miles wasn't finished. He handed her a Bible, too. "Vince might need this," he said.

Tamara merely nodded as she stuck it under her arm and headed for the exit. Vince stood inside the glass foyer. She started walking faster. He'd changed his mind and waited for her! It made no sense, this feeling of gladness, yet it quickened her step.

"I'm right here," she said, but Vince wasn't looking at her.

"Those are storm clouds," he said. Outside, the wind blew unruly leaves across the ground. Only a few people hurried through the parking lot. No one stopped in idle chatter.

"I'm not surprised," Tamara said. "It's looked like rain all day."

"I'm not talking rain. I'm talking tornado weather." He took out his phone and dialed a number. He didn't say a word, just listened. When he clicked off, he shrugged. "There's no mention of a tornado watch. Can I talk you into going home or better yet, heading for your sister's? She shouldn't be alone in this weather."

"She's not alone. Alex took off work this week to stay home with her, to take care of her."

"Then, you're still heading for the church?" Vince asked.

"Yes."

"I might as well start there. My little brother seems to be making it a second home."

Tamara fell in step beside him. "What made you think to ask about Drew's phone? I mean, why wouldn't Jimmy have the phone on him?"

"Drew's in the hospital, so he's not going to call. Jimmy isn't going to use that phone for anything but talking to Drew. He's terrified of Drew."

"If he's terrified of Drew, why is he helping Drew?"

"Money." Vince looked thoughtful. "Jimmy really wants a car, and Drew really wants you gone."

"Then, if we find Jimmy and he tells the truth, this is over."

"Looks that way."

"Seems like Drew's gone to a lot of trouble to cover up a fifty-year-old crime concerning stolen antiques. I wonder why your uncle kept the antique Bible and things. I mean, why did he go to all the trouble of stealing them just to let them languish?" Tamara questioned.

"It's something we can ask him. He might have taken them and held on to them waiting for the right time to sell. Back then he was in and out of trouble so much, he probably forgot all about them in between jail and rehab."

"And all that time, Gloria's family blamed the Griffins."

"Maybe that's what Drew wanted. He might have taken those items for spite. Drew never made anything easy."

"You think Drew still has enough presence to threaten Jimmy?" Tamara asked. "I mean, Jimmy's a teenager, pretty tough-looking."

"Yes, Drew still has enough presence. Drew's physical abilities have diminished, but his mental abilities haven't. Drew's been in Jimmy's nightmares almost all his life. Used to be, when Drew came by, Jimmy hid under the bed. Some things don't improve with age. Drew is one of them."

"If Jimmy's afraid of him, would money be enough to motivate him to work for Drew?"

"If Tommy Skinley's involved, maybe. I'll get ahold of Tommy, either that or the sheriff will. One way or another, we'll figure this out. Truth, there's not much Jimmy wouldn't do to get Drew to leave him alone. It's easier to say yes to Drew than no. Hey, why are you giving me the preacher's Bible?"

"He said to give it to you."

"It's probably a mistake." Vince sighed. "Or considering our dear preacher, maybe it's on purpose." Vince laughed for a moment. "My uncle had one worth thousands of dollars for over fifty years and never read a word. I'll make sure it doesn't take me fifty years to return this one."

Tamara said, "You think he didn't know the worth?"

Vince didn't answer.

"We seem to have forgotten that he said he wants to keep Lydia safe," Tamara continued. "Maybe she stole the Bible stuff and he's trying to cover for her."

Vince stopped by her car, held out his hand and took her keys. He opened the door and saw her in. "That doesn't explain why the stuff would be in his shed. We'll worry about Lydia later. Drive straight to the church. I'll follow right behind you."

"You don't need to follow me. No one's after me. Remember, it's probably Jimmy."

"Jimmy's not responsible for the storm clouds.

They're so low I can feel them." As if to prove his words, a raindrop fell. Then another. And another. Tamara stopped protesting and got into her car, for the first time thinking about what Vince and the sheriff had said about Sherman being in Tornado Alley.

Right now, the town looked asleep in the gray rain. Tamara's windshield wipers did little against the on-slaught. When she finally parked in the church's parking lot, the skies opened up to a full-blown waterfall instead of a light shower. Vince was out of his truck, fumbling around behind the seat for a minute, and then running toward her. He had a flashlight and a jacket, which he quickly draped over the top of her head as they ran for the front door. She pulled the key from her purse and opened the door to a room as gray as the outdoors.

Vince pushed her in and quickly closed the door. He took out his phone and dialed a number and listened for a moment. "We have a watch now."

"What does that mean?"

"It means the conditions are right for a tornado, but one hasn't been spotted." He turned on the light and started going around the room checking windows. Tamara took a moment to wipe the rain from her eyes, and then went into the kitchen and classrooms and started helping him. They saved the upstairs for last.

The contents of the second box were spread across the floor.

"I've been putting the bulletins in order based on the dates. Then, I started reading, specifically looking for information about Lorraine and Lydia."

"What'd you find?" The crack of thunder rumbled low and long. The lights flickered.

Tamara shivered before saying, "I wish I could have

met Lorraine. She seemed like a real go-getter. Everything I came across had her doing things for other people. Meanwhile, Lydia was a live wire. She ran away from home, went into counseling, and got pregnant before she graduated high school."

"Lots of people run away, go into counseling, and start a family before they really mean to. That only means she had a rough time finding herself. Plus, if she got messed up with Drew, no wonder her life was such a mess."

"But—"

"Wait until you meet her. You'll see. She learned from her mistakes. Drew never did."

Tamara shivered again, but it wasn't from cold. She wanted to meet Lorraine, find out about someone who seemed so good. Yet, here was Vince, talking about Lydia, who made so many mistakes, terrible mistakes, and then changed.

Tamara had always been afraid to make mistakes.

The lights flickered again and finally went out. Vince pulled the flashlight from his belt and headed for the window.

"What time is it?" Tamara asked.

"It's not even four."

Tamara came to stand beside him. The attic suddenly wasn't her favorite place. It was too high up, too vulnerable. "Look how dark it is."

"You have anything in the car you need?"

"What do you mean?"

"I mean we're heading down to the storm cellar. I don't need to call the weather channel to see a watch turning into a warning."

"Do I need to be scared?"

He moved with a fluid grace she wasn't expecting,

and in a moment she found herself enveloped in his arms, safe in his arms. "You don't need to be scared when you're with me."

For a moment, she leaned into him and believed, but then the wind picked up with a slight whistle that turned into a sinister hum. Her heart quickened. His arms tightened around her, offering comfort, yet again he wasn't looking at her. He was watching the clouds. "We're going to the storm cellar now. Nothing in your car is important." He held her hand—tightly as if he were afraid to let go—all the way down the stairs, out the back door, and to a storm cellar door that looked older than the church. The wind sent chills under Tamara's black jacket, and the rain pelted against her black-and-white-striped shirt and plain black slacks.

She held on to his arm, not because she was in danger of blowing away, but because she was amazed by it all—the wind, the rain, the ominous clouds, this man beside her who seemed to know what to do come any situation.

"I'm going to have to get a crowbar," Vince shouted. "It's been some time since this door has been opened."

As he ran back to his truck, Tamara went to her knees and tried to pry the latch open. It had corroded in places and the latch looked somewhat melded to the lock. All she succeeded in doing was getting dirt on her knees and some grayish black resin on her fingers.

"Move," Vince shouted. He did something with the crowbar and then threw open the green door. It only took him a minute. Then he tugged her downstairs into a large room, stale with age and neglect. Rain followed, as if angry that they were escaping. Vince closed the doors and only the chill of a disappearing wind remained.

The beam from his flashlight barely made a dent in the fluid darkness as Vince perused the room. Shelves lined three walls. They were empty except for a few dishes and cobwebs. The final wall had an old door leaning against it. Next to that were a ladder, some old tarps or blankets, and a number of folding chairs.

"How wet are you?" he asked.

"Not much at all."

"Good, because we're going to be down here a while." He shone the beam high and low, finally taking it to the wall and the old folding chairs. The first three he tried to open were either broken beyond use or jammed shut. The final two worked. He positioned them in the middle of the room on the dirt floor.

Tamara took a seat, unmindful of their condition. "Have you ever been down here before?" Tamara asked.

"No need. I don't think Lydia's been down here in many years either." He took out his cell phone, looked at it and muttered, "No service." He paced the room, searching every corner. Tamara watched, liking what she saw, and believing he'd keep her safe.

Funny how safe she felt.

"Used to be," Vince said, "people stocked their storm cellars. Once we get this place up to speed, we'll do that. Then, if there's ever another warning, you won't be down here with nothing."

"I think one tornado is enough to last a lifetime," Tamara said.

Vince chuckled. "If you're going to call Nebraska home, then you'll need to get used to the weather."

The storm cellar door rattled. For a moment, Tamara thought somebody else was taking refuge from the storm. But Vince didn't make a move to go see what was going on or who was out there. One of the chairs slid to the ground.

Tamara tried not to jump. "How long do tornadoes usually last?"

"Depends," Vince answered. "It could be minutes, could be hours. If there really is one, it's not here yet. The wind will let us know. If you think that storm door almost opened just now, wait and see what it does if a tornado really does drive by."

"You mean all this could be just heavy wind?"

"Let's pray all this is heavy wind."

"Pray?" Tamara looked at the serious expression on his face. "Almost sounds as if you really think prayer might help."

"Even if it's just a chance, I'll willingly pray that a tornado passes us by."

The storm door shook again, this time banging a little as it rose and lowered. The hum outdoors increased, getting faster and louder. Vince looked around the room. "If we were at my place, we'd be under some mattresses. That won't work here." He walked over and moved the table and some of the other chairs. Dust flew and a moldy old blanket fell to the ground.

Tamara didn't care. She followed him. She'd touch the moldy old blanket. She'd even risk her nails if there was something for her to do, something to keep her mind off the never-ending sound of the wind. "What can I do to help?"

He kicked the blanket aside. "I thought I'd angle this table so we could get behind it if… Hmm, what's this?" He crouched down, shoving the blanket aside. Tamara had to tug the table away in order to see.

"Looks like some sort of hatch." Vince brushed away debris and dirt, uncovering an opening. "It's made of steel or something, but why is it down here?"

"I know what it is," Tamara whispered. "It's a fallout shelter. Remember, the bulletin talked about President Kennedy advising people to have one. With all the other nooks and crannies this place has, it's no surprise to find one down here."

"A fallout shelter? I've never seen one," Vince said. "Maybe it's an answer to that prayer. Let's hope I can open it. It'd be perfect right about now."

It took him over five agonizing minutes to twist the knob on the top. His knuckles turned red from the effort. Outside the storm intensified. The storm cellar door rattled. Something fell. About the time Tamara thought the building just might collapse, the hatch finally opened. The space revealed only darkness. Vince aimed the beam of his flashlight down. "I don't see any steps. Let me make sure it's safe." Vince pushed a piece of wood through the opening. Its landing made a soft thud after only a moment.

"It's a short drop," Vince said. "I'm sure I can get in and back out."

Tamara wanted to protest. What if he dropped into the hole and broke his leg? Or what if he dropped into the hole and just kept dropping?

Leaving her alone.

Upstairs something fell over. The sound echoed and then was buried under a wind that Tamara knew could move the building like Dorothy's Oz. Glass broke. Vince scooted into the hole, lowering himself slowly, all the while maintaining a firm grip on the opening, before finally letting go. He dropped a short distance before she heard him hit ground and say, "Hand me the flashlight."

She aimed it down. She didn't see his hand reaching, but she saw the top of his head. He apparently could see her, because when she reached down with the flashlight, he took it and stated, "I completely missed seeing the ladder, but wow."

"Wow? Can I come down and see now?" Tamara asked. Any place was better than sitting on a dirt floor with the wind trying to bring down the walls around your head.

Then, everything but the drip of rain went silent. The sudden change from noise to nothing was worse than the noise. Without waiting for an answer, she carefully backed into the hole and felt for the ladder before joining him as he flicked the flashlight from one end of the room to the other.

There was no dust in this room. It was clean and barren in its simplicity although it smelled of age, mildew and mostly a strong sickly odor that Tamara figured was left over from the remains of canned goods lining one concrete wall. Some were still intact; others were black. Some were tipped over and only brown smudges remained of the contents.

Water storage containers lined another wall. A table and two chairs were in the middle of the room. A box with lanterns and candles waited in the middle. Vince walked over, set his flashlight faceup on the table, and in just a minute he had two glowing lanterns hanging from hooks at each end of the room.

A bunk bed occupied a side wall. Blankets and pillows were scattered haphazardly over the bottom bunk. The top bunk housed neatly stacked books and more than a dozen board games. Tamara walked over and looked at the titles of the books. "They're not religious books," she announced.

"And obviously the minister wasn't thinking about saving the whole church," Vince said. "Four might be comfortable, but six would be a crowd in this room."

"I think this room predates the church. Remember, it was Lydia's uncle who first lived here. He's the one who loved the hidey-holes and such."

Upstairs the storm door rattled again and a low roar bellowed into the storm cellar. Tamara turned, bumping into Vince, and his arms went around her, pulling her close. He was somewhat damp from the rain, and there was a smudge of dirt on his cheek, but he looked good and felt good, and he was the only thing keeping her together at the moment.

"We're going to be just fine," he murmured into her hair.

"It smells down here," Tamara said.

"We'll get used to it."

"What if the hatch closes—we'll be trapped."

"I'm going to close the hatch, and when it's time to leave, I'll open it again."

When she didn't say anything else, he added, "I promise."

She didn't move, just stayed nestled in his embrace. Finally, she looked up at him. "You take care of everybody, you know that? You act like you're this happy-go-lucky bachelor, but you're really a big old bear who takes care of everyone. I think I first realized that when you sat next to me at the hospital and talked about watching over an uncle who certainly never watched out for you."

"I don't willingly watch over my uncle. It's more unwillingly. And my uncle's the reason we're in this mess."

"He didn't cause the tornado."

"No, but he's probably part of the reason this building

has been in disrepair for so long, and why we haven't made more headway."

"I'm not mad at your uncle," Tamara whispered.

Vince's fingers bit into her shoulders, almost immediately he released them. "How can you not be mad at my uncle? He ruins everything."

"If not for your uncle, you never would have stopped that first day…" She wanted to go on, tell him exactly what his support had meant to her, but the look on his face stopped her.

He didn't care. She could babble about feelings for the next hour, and he still wouldn't get it. Like every other man in her life, he walked away.

He couldn't go far.

Only as far as the open hatch.

He climbed the ladder, stuck his head out the opening and listened for a minute. "The wind is starting back up. I think we just went through the eye of the storm. We're in the center of the storm now."

He closed the hatch and climbed back down. He walked over to the shelves with canned goods and military rations. Picking up a can, he said, "Expired in 1963. This place was a church then."

"Canned goods last for years before they expire. Those could have been purchased in the late fifties."

"Whoever put this room together was a craftsman. Everything is sized perfectly and in its place. No wasted space yet enough room."

"I'm not sure how long people expected they'd have to live in their fallout shelters should they have to use them," Tamara said. She pulled one of the table chairs out and sat down.

"Maybe you should have been a policeman," she

joked, while watching him investigate the room. "You're nosy enough."

"Not as nosy as a lawyer."

"I'm beginning to think there's a lot to be said about people who work with their hands."

He finally turned and looked at her. What she wanted him to do was say *I'm beginning to think there's a lot to be said about a woman lawyer* as he looked at her. But men never said that to Tamara. Sheila claimed it was because most men were afraid.

Near as Tamara could tell, Vince wasn't afraid of anything.

Tamara used to be that way.

He went back to studying the room. He wound up in front of the bunk bed, fingering the dusty books and tapping the game boxes. "I know how to play this. Don't know how to play this. Know how to play this."

One of the games slipped from his finger. Vince moved to catch it. His knee brushed against a blanket hanging off the edge of the lower bunk. It slid to the floor, revealing the skeletal remains of a hand.

THIRTEEN

Vince didn't move. Ivory-brown fingers—splayed open, lying stark against a brown blanket—were all he could focus on.

A hand, a human hand.

He couldn't seem to look away. No matter how he tried.

"Don't touch anything," Tamara ordered.

Vince stepped backward.

"Stop!" Tamara ordered, "You don't want to compromise the crime scene. There's probably still trace samples left and—"

Vince held up his hand. He wasn't sure he even wanted to know what trace samples were, and he had every intention of stopping. There was something so wrong in disturbing someone's final resting place.

"How do you know it's a crime scene?" he asked.

She looked around the room, at the floor and the ceiling, and finally said, "I just know. Call it lawyerly intuition. Lately my whole life has been a crime scene."

He couldn't argue with that. She was scared, and she was between a rock and a hard place—tornado above, fallout shelter with a dead body below. He stepped away, intending to follow her advice, leave well enough alone. Instead, his foot tangled in the blanket and it fell away.

Behind him, he heard Tamara squeak.

As for Vince, he couldn't move, only stare. The brown skull still had a few strands of hair. The head was tilted to the side as if querying Vince as to why he'd interrupted its slumber. One hand was over its chest; the other draped to the ground.

"It was a female."

"Don't call her an it," Tamara said.

Vince was comfortable with *it; her* seemed too real.

The body wore white go-go boots and a green and white beaded belt.

He looked back at Tamara. "Maybe it's a transient. Someone who lost her way…"

"I don't think so." Tamara still made no move to leave the "safe" zone under the hatch. "I doubt very much that she was alive when she was put in that bed."

"Put?" Vince looked at the bed.

"If she were a transient and gave up, I'd think she'd be curled up in a fetal position," Tamara said.

"So you think she was put here?"

"I do, and I think we should go up and see how the weather is."

Tamara started up the ladder and Vince followed.

"When were go-go boots popular? I'm thinking the fifties and sixties?" he wondered.

"You're thinking right," Tamara agreed. "Go-go boots and fallout shelters were both popular." She'd only managed to climb one ladder rung.

"In the sixties, this place was a church." Vince stepped closer.

Tamara nodded and slowly climbed two more rungs. "In the sixties, Lydia's sister ran away," she said, just shy of the opening. Then Tamara moved. She had the hatch open and pulled herself out of the fallout shelter before Vince had time to look back at the corpse. "I'm thinking she didn't run far."

"I think you're right," Vince said. "But she'd know about the fallout shelter, so maybe what we just stumbled across was a natural death."

"There's nothing natural about dying in a fallout shelter that not only contains a way out but which has food and water."

"So, you think we're looking at a murder." He said the words slowly, not liking the sound, and not liking his next thought. "That certainly explains why someone wanted you out of here."

"It also," Tamara said, "might explain why the Griffins kicked the church congregation out and then why the place was empty so long."

Vince knew what Tamara was implying. He tried to wrap his mind around the thought that Lydia knew her sister was down here. Impossible was what he wanted to say, but he didn't need a law degree to understand probable. He pulled himself out of the hole. He'd forgotten to grab either his flashlight or any of the lanterns, but he didn't need them, because someone was lifting the storm cellar door.

Tamara's brother-in-law soon stood in the opening. His face was white. "I've been looking for you for an hour."

"We haven't been down here for that long," Tamara protested.

"No, but it's been an hour since Lisa went into labor."

"Why aren't you with her?" Tamara exclaimed. "She needs you more than I do!"

"I thought so, too, until the tornado sirens went off and you weren't at your apartment and I couldn't reach you by phone. I knew Lisa'd have my hide if I showed up and didn't know if you were okay."

"Where were you during the tornado?" Vince asked.

"In one of the bathrooms," Alex said. "It hit right when I got here. Believe me, if I'd known about the storm cellar I'd have been down here with you. I've never been caught in anything quite like this."

"Anything damaged?" Tamara headed for Alex.

"No, just some trees down and lots of debris, at least here. I'm anxious to get to the hospital. Come on."

Vince took his phone out. Good, he had service. He dialed 911. It took him only a moment to give the Amhurst Church address and report a dead body. Looking at the trees, mud and fallen telephone lines, he emphasized that the dead body had been there for years and there was no hurry. Throughout Sherman, there'd be others who needed immediate help.

He glanced up from his phone and watched as Tamara circled her little car. The old weathervane from atop the church had landed on the hood with such force that it looked like Mother Nature had shot an arrow.

"That'll be hard to fix," Alex said as he jogged to his truck. "You want to ride with me."

"No, I'll ride with Vince."

Alex grinned and jumped behind the wheel.

"Soon," Vince said, "people will start to talk."

"Yeah, and if my guess is right, they'll be talking about the body in the fallout shelter. They'll be talking about Lorraine Griffin and who killed her."

It sobered Vince. She wasn't even remembering what he remembered. The words his uncle had said.

I'm keeping Lydia safe.

Just what had Lydia done?

* * *

"It's Lorraine," Tamara said. "I just know it's Lorraine."

"I think so, too. It makes so much sense."

"Why did her family keep her disappearance a secret? Now that makes no sense. All these years, no one's been looking for her. She's been down there *alone*. I've been thinking while I worked up in the attic. I read so much about her. I truly believed she'd given up on her family and decided to start a new life somewhere else."

"I wish we hadn't found her," Vince said.

"No, she deserves more than this. She deserves a decent burial."

"It's going to be up to Billy, then. He's the only family she has left. Lydia's not up to making the arrangements."

Tamara watched his face. "You're worried Lydia did it," she said.

His lips tightened. It was the only sign he gave that she'd hit a nerve.

"Well," she continued, "it makes sense. If Lydia killed her sister, what better place to hide the body. They'd been in this church back when it was a house. They'd know all the secret places their uncle created."

Vince's fingers tightened on the steering wheel.

"The law is probably not going to try to prosecute," Tamara said gently. "We're talking about a fifty-year-old murder with an elderly and ill possible murder suspect."

He didn't look comforted.

"Maybe it was self-defense?" Tamara suggested. "We know Lydia was going through a tough period. Maybe Lorraine was in the wrong place at the wrong time, and her sister—"

"If it were self-defense, why hide the body? Why keep a church empty for decades? And if Lydia did indeed do it, which I doubt, that still doesn't explain who is trying to scare you away from the church."

"Oh, you're right. Maybe not Lydia."

The hospital came into view. Tamara sat up. "Maybe it's Gloria. She was angry at the Griffins for turning her dad out of the church."

"Didn't we figure that Gloria was eight or nine in 1962?" Vince countered. "That's a little young to be committing murder, and probably it took her a while to work up..." His voice tapered off.

"What are you thinking?"

"That's why the Griffins kicked everyone out of the church. Gloria isn't the killer. She didn't have a motive until *after* Lorraine was murdered. The killer must have been Lorraine's mother or father. They hid her in the fallout shelter and then forced everyone out of the old church. Drew keeps nosing around, but if he were the murderer, he would have buried her and the Griffins would not have been involved."

The hospital's parking lot was full, as was the street in front. Vince parked a full block away, and they hurried to the entrance.

"Trust my sister to choose the day a tornado hits to have her baby."

Vince didn't laugh. "This will certainly be a day we remember."

It would be a day the town would remember, too. Right inside the entryway, sitting on a bench, were Vince's mother and little brother. Debbie Billingsby held a towel to Jimmy's head. Blood covered his shirt.

Vince stopped so quickly that Tamara bumped into the back of him.

"What happened?" he exclaimed.

"Head wounds always bleed a lot," Tamara said. "Calm down."

"I'm not calming down." He looked at his mother, and she slowly shook her head. For a moment, Tamara didn't get the exchange, but then she saw the anger spark in Vince's eyes.

"Still using the red paint out of Drew's shed, Jimmy?"

Before Jimmy could answer, Tamara's cell phone sounded. Vince's fingers closed into a tight fist.

Tamara held the phone away from her ear. Vince could hear an excited Alex screaming, "You need to get up here! You need to get up here!"

Tamara didn't need another prompt. Her expression went from pensive to gleeful. "Lisa's having her baby, let's go."

"You go," Vince said. "I need to stay here."

She didn't move. She clutched the phone, and the look on her face was full of expectations—expectations Vince had no business trying to fulfill. Only on television did people from two different sides of the track find happily ever after together.

Alex was still talking. Vince figured he was telecasting every single moment of his son's arrival. Alex was a man who knew how to fulfill expectations, not Vince.

"I…" Tamara looked uncertain for only a moment. Then she clicked off the phone and said, "I need you to come with me." She reached for his hand. He let her take it but made no move to return the caress.

"I *want* you to come with me," she repeated.

He saw it in her eyes. Throughout this whole mess, they'd pretty much toughed it out together. Glancing at his baby brother, Vince couldn't help but wonder how long it would be before Tamara realized that it had been his family pulling the puppet strings—his family responsible for her pain.

"No, I need to stay here. I want to talk with my brother."

She didn't nod, didn't shake her head, but stood watching him. She never looked at his brother or mother. She only looked at him, only had expectations for him. It appeared Tamara didn't care, or maybe didn't realize, the truth behind what was going on.

"I'll call you." Tamara held up her cell phone.

"Do that," Vince answered.

When his cell phone sounded, and her name appeared, he wouldn't answer.

"So," Vince said after Tamara walked away, "I'll take your nonanswer about the paint as a yes. How did you get the bump on your head?"

"He and Tommy Skinley got in a fight," Debbie supplied.

"Why?"

"Lots of things," Jimmy sneered.

"Like Tommy throwing glass bottles at my car? Like what you've been doing for Drew?"

Jimmy didn't answer.

Debbie's lips pressed together. "They were at the old park west of Main Street. You kids used to play there when we rented that old house with just one bedroom."

Vince barely remembered the house. What he did remember was hanging at the park…he'd been there recently, too, scaring his brother home, and trying to talk sense into Tommy Skinley.

"Were you painting something before the tornado hit?"

Jimmy didn't answer.

"The sheriff stopped by the house before the watch

began," Debbie said. "He had some pictures. Some were of your girlfriend's new office and what had been painted there. The rest were of Gloria Baker's front door. He'd been to the high school looking for ideas on which kids like all those Japanese drawings, which kids were suspected of doing graffiti. I guess Tommy Skinley's name came up, and wherever Tommy is, Jimmy is."

"Only this time," Vince said, "it's more like wherever Jimmy is, Tommy is. How much is Drew paying you?"

Jimmy sat up and glared. "You don't even care that I'm hurt."

"I know about the cell phone. Mom found it this morning."

"What cell phone?" Jimmy protested. "Everyone has a cell phone."

"Not everyone has two, and not everyone has a cell phone with just a few calls logged and all to and from the same number."

"You had no right—" Jimmy protested.

"Oh, it wasn't me." Vince shook his head. "The sheriff was already looking into that angle. No doubt it helped him know what questions to ask when he got to the high school."

Jimmy moaned, whether it was really a headache or that he considered Vince a headache, Vince didn't know. What Vince did know was that Drew had somehow gotten to Jimmy, either by money or threats.

An ambulance roared up to the emergency-room doors. Vince backed out of the way and watched as two paramedics efficiently pulled a gurney from the back of the ambulance and wheeled it in.

Before Vince could turn back to Jimmy, another ambulance came up. Sherman only had two, which told Vince exactly how much damage the tornado had done. No wonder Gloria Baker harped about having a hospital room out of commission. She thought of the future; Vince had only thought of the present.

It was why he was still single.

Once the paramedics carted another victim in, Vince told his mother, "I'm heading up to see Drew. Maybe he'll be conscious enough to talk."

Jimmy managed to turn his sullen expression into one of deep, dark depression. Judging by how their mother barely noticed, Vince figured his brother had been utilizing that look for some time.

When Vince finally made it to Drew's room his temper had cooled. Good thing, because Drew was awake. His eyes were bright and followed Vince into the room. The man didn't blink.

"I've spent an interesting afternoon over at the church," Vince said. "Tamara pulled into the parking lot at about the same time as the tornado.

"We went down into the storm cellar. Thought I'd never get the door open. Bet you couldn't open it. Huh? Have you tried lately? It's a dark, dirty place. No one's been down there for years, decades even."

Another blink from Drew, but no facial expression, not even the wrinkling of a nose. One foot, the left, twitched.

"Guess what we found?" Vince didn't expect an answer, but he waited anyway, just in case.

"You shouldn't be bothering me," Drew said, his voice surprisingly strong. "There's nothing down there that concerns me."

"Nothing?" Vince asked. "Seems to me that the

nothing that doesn't concern you is really a something. What did you mean, Drew, when you said you were keeping Lydia safe? You know about the body down there, in the fallout cellar, don't you?" Vince paused. "It's why you kept trying to scare Tamara away. Something happened to Lorraine Griffin and you were involved. Bad enough you ruined your life all those years ago, but you had to drag Tamara and Jimmy into this. What kind of man are you?"

Vince didn't wait. He knew the answer. "You're not a man at all."

He strode from the room, mindful that his cell was sounding again. He assumed it was Tamara. Turning the corner, he almost bumped into Miles Pynchon. The minister was trying not to smile. "Did Tamara get ahold of you? She's about ready to burst. She can't seem to stop staring at that niece of hers."

"Niece? I thought Lisa was having a boy?"

"You and the rest of the world."

Vince's phone buzzed again. Taking it from his belt, Vince glanced at the caller and clicked on the answer button. "Yes, Sheriff."

"You disturb the body?"

"I bumped into the bottom bunk when I was looking at the board games on the top. A blanket fell off and there she was, but I didn't touch anything. Tamara made sure of that. Is it Lorraine Griffin?"

"Wouldn't surprise me," the sheriff said. "The remains look old enough, and it's her identification in the purse. Can you and Tamara head back here?"

"Tamara's with her sister." Vince paused. That wasn't quite true. Tamara was speed walking down the hall toward them. "I take that back. Tamara and the preacher are here with me. We're standing outside Drew's hospital room. I tried to get him to tell me what he knows, and believe me, I know he knows something, but all he does is talk about Lydia."

"Maybe it's time I had a talk with her," the sheriff said.

"Tamara and I have been trying to get in and talk to Lydia all week. Each time, they tell us she's not doing well."

Who are you talking to? Tamara mouthed.

"The sheriff," Miles answered.

Before Vince could say anything else, the sheriff hung up, leaving Vince with the uncomfortable feeling they were on the same side.

"Boy!"

They all jumped. Amidst the noise of an overactive hospital, Drew's gravelly, sharp command had the effect of a bomb.

Vince went back into his uncle's room. The minister and Tamara followed.

"What did I just hear you say?" Drew demanded. "Did I hear you say you've been trying all week to see Lydia?"

"Yes, Uncle Drew, but she's still in the nursing home, and so far hasn't been up to visitors."

Drew shook his head and managed to free his arms from under the blanket. Skin hung from his bones. Age spots peppered from fingertips to just below the sleeve line. Drew trembled with effort, but managed to push himself upright and growl, "You leave Lydia alone. She deserved everything she got. She won't be telling anyone stories."

FOURTEEN

"Drew," Miles said patiently, "she's not telling any stories. Lydia's fine. I saw her just yesterday."

"You got in to see her?" Tamara asked. "We've been trying for over a week. They keep telling us she's not up to visitors."

"I'm pretty sure that's what Billy instructed them to say. I don't think he thinks she's up for visitors. He's been treating her as if she's fragile glass."

"Billy's here?" Drew asked.

"Yes," Miles answered. "He got here on Wednesday. He's living right below you, Tamara."

"You're kidding. There's no new car out front. I haven't heard him."

"He's letting one of his daughters back in Denver use his car while he's here. As little as you're home and as much as he's with his mother, it's no surprise you haven't bumped into each other," Miles said.

"What does Billy look like?" Drew asked. "Lydia always kept him from me. I don't remember him ever coming here."

Tamara said, "I haven't seen him since I signed the final papers, but he's a fairly stocky, dark-haired man.

He has a wife and two children, both grown with families of their own. He was a restaurant manager. I think he quit a few weeks ago. Probably so he could come here and take care of his mother."

Drew visibly shuddered.

"Are you all right?" Miles asked.

"Git," Drew said. "Just git. Now!"

"Mr. Frenci." Miles moved to the side of Drew's bed. "Calm down. I assure you, Lydia's all right. She's getting stronger every day."

One of the machines Drew was hooked up to started beeping. Any other day, a nurse would be hustling in, but thanks to the tornado, the nurses were already hustling. Still, no matter what she and Vince were feeling about this vile man, getting him overstimulated—especially at his age—was not a good idea.

She put her hand on Vince's sleeve. "We need to let your uncle rest. Let's go see Lydia."

As she herded the men from the room, she could hear the faint sound of Drew moaning, "Nooooo."

Miles was the only one who looked back. "Should I stay with him?"

"Trust me," Vince said. "When he's like this, it's best to leave him alone."

"He's been alone all his life, hasn't he?" Miles asked.

Tamara looked at Vince.

"Not all his life," Vince said gruffly. "He's managed to involve himself in my family. Thanks to Drew, Jimmy's starting his own rap sheet. The red paint on the shirt he's wearing will probably match the paint from your door, Tamara."

"It's from today," Tamara figured out. "From painting on Gloria Baker's door."

"Probably on Drew's orders and dime. That old man's alert enough to keep track—thanks to Jimmy—of what's going on. Jimmy must have told him about our visit to her house." Vince shook his head.

"But why would your visit to Gloria upset Drew?" Miles asked.

When Vince didn't answer, Tamara filled in, "Gloria's probably one of the few people who knows that Drew is Billy's father."

Never had Tamara seen the minister at a loss for words, and she'd seen him numerous times, but now his mouth opened and nothing came out.

"It gets worse," Vince said. "You heard my conversation with the sheriff, right?"

Miles nodded.

"Then you've probably figured out that earlier today Tamara and I found a body."

"Lorraine Griffin's, maybe," Miles said.

"We're pretty sure—" Vince looked at Tamara "—and we're pretty sure that Drew has something to do with her death. That's why he's worked so hard to scare Tamara away from the church."

For a moment Vince's featured softened. Tamara doubted anyone else would have noticed.

"Only Tamara doesn't scare easily."

"I had you beside me," Tamara said. "You made it easy not to be so scared."

Vince shook his head, and she knew he was going right back to their earlier discussion, that she couldn't be impressed with his help if the danger came from *his* family. She tried to think of something to say, but before she could, he said, "You stepped up right when the sheriff hung up. We probably need to head over there, first."

"I'm surprised he's there, what with the tornado and all the people who need help." Miles looked around the hospital hallway. "But then, the tornado didn't touch down," Miles continued, "at least not according to the weather station. What you see downstairs is mostly posttornado, from rescue and cleanup attempts."

"Both ambulances seemed pretty busy," Vince remarked.

"Oh, no doubt the high winds and falling debris have wreaked havoc on Sherman, but a dead body takes precedence," Tamara said.

"Do you mind if I come with you?" Miles asked. "If the body, indeed, is Lorraine, then I want to be there when they break the news to Lydia."

"It might not be for a while," Tamara warned. "It takes time to prove identity."

Miles shook his head. "Already, at least three people believe Lorraine Griffin has been discovered. By Sunday services, the whole town will be speculating."

"He's right," Vince said. "And we still need to figure out what Drew meant by keeping Lydia safe. How does keeping Lorraine's body a secret keep Lydia safe?"

"Maybe," Tamara said gently, "he still has a place for Lydia in his heart and knows that finding Lorraine's body will hurt her—especially if Drew had something to do with the death."

Miles took his own vehicle. Tamara climbed into Vince's truck and back to the old church they went. The rain had somewhat diminished, and people were already outside their homes, sweeping up leaves and, in some cases, putting plastic over newly broken windows.

"What do you think? How does all this tie together?"

Tamara asked. "I've never seen anything like it. It's a fifty-year-murder with a present-day twist."

"What I'm remembering is my dad saying Drew wasn't the same when he came back from Vietnam, and that maybe 1962 is about the time Drew came home."

"Twisted and sick?"

"Twisted and sick," Vince agreed.

"Do you think he was twisted and sick when he and Lydia first got together?"

"Maybe not so much. I mean, I'm sitting here thinking about the math. Lydia must have been just out of high school, and Drew might have been on leave or maybe even discharged. He had to be more than ten years older than her, but that's not a surprise. Remember, the Lydia you've told me about sowed a few wild oats of her own. Gloria didn't seem to know if they were a couple, per se. Surely, someone around is from that era. I really am looking forward to talking to Lydia. And in the end, what I want to know about most is Lorraine."

Tamara gasped. "I can't believe I missed this earlier."

"What?"

"We were trying to figure out who owned the church and how Billy was able to sell it. We kept coming across a trust owned by a foundation named Lylo. Remember?"

"I remember. I have checks made out by the foundation."

"Lylo. It's the first two letters of each of their names—Lydia and Lorraine."

"So, Main Street is still owned by the Griffin family?"

"Looks that way," Tamara said, "with Billy being the final shareholder if Lydia is deemed incompetent."

Three cars were in Tamara's parking lot. The first was her damaged Jaguar. It was parked neatly in a space. The sheriff's SUV was smack-dab in the middle of the parking lot. A dark blue Nissan was next to it.

"That poor CSI guy might as well rent a room," Tamara remarked.

"There's certainly not been a dull moment since you moved to town," Vince agreed.

The storm cellar door was open and already cordoned off. Vince led the way, holding out his hand to Tamara. Lamps were set up in the cellar. The fallout shelter hatch was open and muted voices came from below.

The CSI technician had his equipment on the ground by the body. His gloves were on and he was talking into a recorder. The blanket that had been covering Lorraine was in a large bag. The contents from her purse, the belt and other items were in smaller bags. There were quite a few.

Vince stepped closer and studied one. "Where's this zipper from?"

"It's probably left from a winter coat," the CSI guy said. His voice still sounded as if he was dictating.

"What all was in the purse?" Tamara asked.

The CSI guy exchanged a look with Jake. Jake gave a slight nod.

"Identification belongs to Lorraine Griffin. There's a driver's license, but that's all that outright identifies her. There's a lipstick, some loose change, two pens, a diaphragm, a brush. She carried a tiny notebook, but the writing is so faded we'll never be able to read what it says."

"Can I come down?" The preacher's voice sounded from the hatch.

"No," Jake ordered. He looked at Tamara and Vince as he headed for the ladder.

"Miles was standing there when you called," Vince supplied. "We were right outside Drew's hospital room. And if this is Lorraine, Lydia's gonna need Miles's help."

"I'm glad you admit I'm a help," Miles called down.

"A help for Lydia," Vince responded.

"Oh," Jake said as he climbed the ladder, "Miles is a pretty good help in any situation."

After a moment, Jake returned, without Miles, and for the next hour, as the skies outside grew darker, and as rain finally stilled to a heavy dampness, Tamara and Vince reenacted their every move.

Finally, they were allowed to leave.

Down in the fallout shelter, the medical examiner readied Lorraine Griffin's corpse so that it, too, could finally leave.

Friday morning dawned like any other day. Vince's cell phone rang at four. John Konrad, his boss, was putting the hospital job on hold. Thanks to the tornado, Konrad Construction was in high demand. While readying a hospital room was a top priority, getting people back in homes and businesses came first.

Even Gloria Baker would have to agree.

If it were a typical day, Vince would take the day off. He needed to talk with his brother. He needed to talk with Lydia. He needed to make sure Tamara was all right. Calling her at four in the morning wasn't an option. Sometimes, as Vince drove to work in the early morning, he wondered if anyone else was awake.

In the predawn light, Tamara's building rose like a regal gray lady. She was missing the peak of her crown. Tamara's little red car was wearing it instead. Except for the weathervane in the hood and the cordon tape, though, Tamara's place appeared unscathed.

Yano's, across the street, was a different story. A telephone pole had crushed one corner of the building. For once, Vince wasn't alone. The telephone company was already hard at work righting the pole and doing something with the wires.

Vince's job was to repair Yano's before any more rain damage occurred. First, he had to look over Tali's attempt to secure the area. Maybe Yano's could still open for lunch.

Tali and Sharon showed up at seven. They both looked like they needed sleep.

"We were here until midnight," Tali said. "Then, our daughter called. We've been there the rest of the night shoveling water from her basement, where a sewage line broke. So, can we open today or are we closed?"

"Which works best for you?" Vince asked.

"Open. The whole neighborhood's talking about the rents being raised. We know what's coming. Combine that with what we've lost both here and at home we're going to be hard up for money."

"I'll have it so you can open tonight," Vince said.

"Thanks."

Heading out to the company truck to get some tools, Vince watched as a blue Chevy Cavalier pulled into the parking lot. He knew the car. It belonged to Tamara's sister. She wouldn't be needing it since she probably had at least two more days in the hospital. Then, Vince truly doubted Lisa would be driving anytime soon, not with a doting husband around.

Tamara stepped from the car.

She didn't notice him, and it gave him a moment to

admire her. The red hair looked darker under the still-hovering storm clouds. The wind had whisked the long strands away from her neck and into the air.

She was shapeless under a brown jacket that she'd buttoned all the way up. Black boots peeked out from under jeans. She grabbed her purse from the passenger's-side seat, tucked it under her arm, and then wheeled around and finally saw him.

Her smile said it all.

He waved, nodded toward Tali's and grabbed his tools. Right now, two worlds were colliding. One, his world, was irrevocably changed. He'd never be the same. A female had taken possession. The other, her world, could not be irrevocably changed. He'd heard from Lisa about how hard Tamara had worked and for how long and against what odds. Right now, the attraction—on both sides—was raging. Maybe it all had to do with the wild ride they were on. But if there was more, and it wasn't the wild ride, then he had to stop now before the Frenci name killed her future in a different way than Drew had killed Lorraine's.

Because that was what Vince believed. After a late night, and two hours sleep, it was the only option.

Keeping Lydia safe.

Not a chance Drew was thinking of someone else, like Tamara hoped.

Not a chance.

Drew had gotten involved with a girl from an affluent family and look what happened.

Vince went back into the restaurant.

At noon, his cell phone sounded. He was covered in grout, sweaty and tired. Tonight, unless another tornado hit, he'd sleep. Every fiber of his being said so. He checked his caller ID, saw the sheriff's name and answered.

"I'm over here with Lydia Griffin. The preacher's here and so is Lydia's son. We've caught her up on all that's been happening at the old church. She seems to think you deserve to be here."

"I'll take my lunch break now."

Tali looked concerned when Jake closed up his toolbox. Vince pointed to his stomach and to his truck.

"I can fix you something to eat," Tali offered. "No charge."

"Appreciate the offer, but I've got something planned. I'll be back in a jiff."

Tali looked out the window. Tamara was exiting the church and looking toward the restaurant. She must have gotten the same phone call from Jake.

"Just don't forget about my restaurant," Tali pleaded.

A moment later, Vince was seated in Lisa Cooke's little Cavalier. Tamara was behind the wheel. Being a passenger was not something Vince did well, but his truck had plastic as a back window and it looked like rain again. But, in all honesty, Tamara, who couldn't have gotten that much more sleep than he, looked ready to face the world.

"It's not that hard to check up on who was in Vietnam and when. Drew arrived there in December of 1961. He left in October of 1962."

"No surprise."

"Lorraine Griffin doesn't even have an Internet presence. Well, at least, our Lorraine Griffin doesn't. Lydia is there, but you've got to dig deep."

"Tali told me that the rent on his restaurant might be going up," Vince said.

"Yeah, I remember Angela mentioning something about her rent going up, too. I'm thinking that Billy's had time to adjust to being a property owner."

"Didn't take him long."

"He managed a restaurant. He has to know some-thing about checks and balances and making money," Tamara said. "I'm wondering why he sold me the old church for so cheap, though."

"Maybe he didn't know he owned the whole street."

"Maybe," Tamara said softly. "But I doubt it."

She drove the way she worked—quickly and effi-ciently. She parked the Cavalier next to the sheriff's SUV in the Sherman Oaks Nursing Home's parking lot.

"I've done some work here," Vince remarked.

"You do get around."

The minister was in the home's lobby getting a soda from the machine. Behind him, four ladies played Scrabble and laughed. Two other women snoozed in wheelchairs. By the far wall, an elderly man read the Sherman newspaper. Even from a distance, Vince could see that the almost-tornado made headline news.

"There will never be another week like this one," Miles said.

"We can only hope," Tamara agreed.

As they followed Miles to the elevator, he said, "Lydia has a private room. Billy saw to that."

"Is Billy in there now?" Tamara asked.

"Yes."

They made it up to the third floor. Green-and-blue-speckled carpeting covered the floor. Portraits deco-rated the walls. A bulletin board requested soup labels for a grandchild and announced birthdays.

"Has Lydia said anything?" Tamara asked.

"She took the news of her sister's death very well, considering. She asked who found the body and what happened afterward. She did seem a bit surprised that you were involved, Vince."

"Really? Because of Drew, you think?"

"I don't know. Jake told her you'd been holed up with Tamara during a tornado and that you'd taken refuge in the storm cellar. If anything, she had more questions about Tamara than she did about Lorraine."

Tamara noticed how each room had a tiny corkboard next to it. The residents' names were written in black marker on white paper. They stopped in front of the room that had a placard with Lydia Griffin written on it. Next to her name was a picture of the cross. In God We Trust was scrawled at the top.

"Do you think she's known all along that her sister's body was down in the fallout shelter?" Vince asked.

"Of course, she did," Tamara said, "or she'd have rented or sold the place a long time ago."

They entered the room. Billy Griffin sat in a chair by his mother's side. A movable table was next to him. A half-finished puzzle was on it. The sheriff leaned against a wall heater. Get-well cards were taped to the wall. A picture of Billy and Lydia was on the nightstand. A picture of Billy, his wife and two kids who looked like they should be in high school was on the dresser.

Lydia's face lit up when she saw Vince. He moved toward her and took one of her hands in his. "I should have stopped by weeks ago. I'm sorry."

"You're a busy boy. You always were." She looked at Tamara. "I saw at the wedding she was keeping you busy. Busy is good."

"I just work for Tamara," Vince protested.

"I bought the old building on Main Street from

Billy." Even as Tamara uttered the words she figured they were needless.

"I sold too soon," Billy said.

"Or maybe you sold just right," Lydia said. "It's time for old secrets to be laid to rest."

"Like your sister should be laid to rest?" Tamara asked.

"Exactly," Lydia responded.

"Mom, are you sure you're up this?" Billy questioned. "You're just starting to get your strength back. The doctor said—"

"The doctor says a lot of things, and they all begin with 'For a woman of your age…'"

"For a woman of your age," Vince said, "you look amazing."

"Flirt." Lydia turned to Tamara. "You have to watch out for him. The Frenci boys have always been charmers."

"Even Drew?" Tamara asked.

The twinkle left Lydia's eyes. "Even Drew."

"He's not a charmer now," Vince said. "I guess he had quite a night. He ranted most of it. My mother called me this morning. The hospital called her. She's heading over there when she gets off work."

Lydia pulled her hand from Vince's and motioned for Billy. "Miles, I need you here, too."

Vince stepped back so Miles could come sit on the side of Lydia's bed. He was so close to Tamara, now, that his arm brushed hers.

He didn't seem to notice.

"You need to know about Drew," Lydia said to Billy.

"Whatever you want to tell me, Mom." Billy looked tired, and older than when he'd sold Tamara the building.

"Drew Frenci is your father."

It was obvious by the look on Billy's face that the name meant nothing to him. Lydia's facial expression soon changed, though, as she looked around the room. "None of you are surprised."

"We've traced Drew to most of the threats and damages Tamara's suffered since she purchased your building," Vince said. "We were looking for his motivation. Gloria Baker remembered that you and Drew were a couple and that Billy was probably his."

"I've always been amazed by how few people remembered. Back then, having a baby out of wedlock meant a black mark that didn't get erased." Lydia never took her eyes off Billy. "I never felt that way. You were the most adorable baby. You had a thick head of hair at birth. It felt so soft. I'd pat it down and it would bounce back up. And smart. You took your first step at eight months. By ten months, you were walking."

"I thought you said you really didn't know my father," Billy said.

"I never believed in lying," Lydia said softly. "Watching my dad do business and hurt people, especially our family, just turned me off. The Bakers, Gloria's mom actually, invited me to church when I was still a young teen. I saw what family was supposed to be. I wanted that life." She looked at Billy. "I wanted that life for you."

"But you lied," Billy said. "All these years, I could have had a father?"

"It's no wonder the Bible says 'Do not lie,'" Lydia said. "Lies have cost so many in this town so much."

"Lydia," Miles said carefully, "our Father forgives and—"

"Miles, tell them what the Bible says after 'Do not lie.'"

"You're being too hard on yourself," Miles said instead. "Even Peter lied and was forgiven."

"In this case," Vince said, "lying was necessary. Drew is not father material. Believe me, he's my great-uncle. Lydia did you a favor by keeping you away from him."

"The Bible goes on to say 'Do not deceive one another.' I didn't lie about not knowing your father. I never knew him *that* way. I lied about something else. Something…" Lydia's bottom lip quivered. "Something that every day of my life, I've prayed about and cried about, but if I had to do it again, lie again, I would, God forgive me."

"Lydia, God hates the sin not the sinner," Miles said.

Tears streaming down her cheeks, Lydia nodded. "Right reasons… Yes. *Turn from evil and do good.* I've told myself that time and time again." She looked at Billy, reaching out and cupping his chin in her hand. "And you are good." She stared in his eyes.

Tamara had been in many a room where two other people suddenly only saw each other. But never before had she *really* understood how it could happen.

"You made me so proud," Lydia said. "And watching you with your wife, going to church every Sunday, working hard at your job and raising those two girls and getting them started in college."

"Mom, you're scaring me."

"I lied, but not about not knowing your father. I didn't really know Drew, that is until my sister got messed up with him, and even then the only reason she did was because she was pregnant with you."

"What?" Billy leaned forward, his hand on Lydia's. "What do you mean your sister was pregnant with me?"

"The diaphragm," Tamara breathed. "It belonged to Lydia. Go-go boots. Lydia would have worn go-go boots. The only thing you changed out was the wallet. You're Lorraine."

"I'm Lorraine. After Lydia died, I took her wallet and I took Billy, and I left Sherman. I didn't come back for almost thirty years."

"Why? Why did you do all that?" Billy asked.

"Because, with my sister dead, the courts would have given Drew custody of you. He was out of work, you'd have been a dependant. Drew always saw the money angle. I couldn't bear to think of you being raised by either him or his parents."

"I don't think there's anyone left who even remembers Drew's parents," Vince said.

"They drank. All the time. You'd come back from their house and say bad words, talk about things little boys shouldn't even know about. Lydia said…" Her voice tapered off.

"Are you all right? Mom?" Billy sat up straight.

"It's just funny to say her name after all these years. Forty years of going by Lydia and suddenly I get to talk about my sister as Lydia again. I loved her, you know. We were twins. We looked the same, but acted nothing alike. We survived many a rough spot."

"I don't understand," Tamara said. "Even in the 1960s the courts would have known Drew wasn't custodial parent material. You worked at the church, you had a college degree, you…"

"There's still one more sin I've had to live with."

This time Lydia looked at Jake.

"It's my fault Lydia died. I…I killed her."

FIFTEEN

"I've never heard such nonsense. What kind of drugs are they giving you here?" Billy looked around the room, as if he hoped someone would second his words.

"It's true," Lydia protested. "I was working late at the church. It was past ten at night, and in came Lydia and Jasper."

Lydia looked at Jake.

Jake stopped leaning and stood. "Are you saying my grandfather is involved with this?"

"He and Lydia were good friends. They always had been, even when he went into law enforcement and she, well, she went into law breaking."

"How did Grandpa wind up with her that night?"

"She'd been acting out at one of the local bars. By the time your grandfather got there, she'd gotten into a fight with another girl, over Drew no less, and had broken a whole tray of glasses while she was running around the bar thinking someone was chasing her. No one was. The owner wanted to press charges. I think your grandfather talked him out of it. He got her out of there and came and found me at the church.

"I'd grown up rescuing her. I let them in. She was

wild-eyed. Her words were garbled. She couldn't even walk right. She was dancing and twirling. Then, out of nowhere, she started laughing hysterically. I can still hear her. Sometimes in my dreams, I can still hear her."

Tamara could sympathize. Sometimes in her dreams she could hear William Massey's voice, all honey—not hysterical. Then, too, she could hear that song he always played about the midnight hour. Lydia Griffin had had her own midnight hour some fifty years ago.

"Jasper and I got her calmed down," Lydia continued.

"You did what you had to do," Billy said. "She was your sister."

"She was *your* mother, and don't doubt this—she loved you. If she'd had the time, she'd have gotten off the drugs and she'd have done right by you. She just ran out of time." Lydia shivered.

Tamara knew it wasn't from the cold, but from the memories.

"Jasper had to get back to the bar. Seemed that night was quite a night. My sister wasn't the only one breaking things. He'd promised the owner he'd come back. We put her in my car. He waved goodbye. I can still remember. At that moment, it was still just a typical night. I ran into the church to get my purse. All I wanted to do was get her home and into bed."

"Where was I?" Billy asked.

"With my mother, your grandmother. You were just past two years old." Lydia reached out and caressed his hair. He suddenly looked young, but Tamara knew he had to be nearing fifty. Maybe it was because even with all that was being dumped on him, the awful truths, he was still looking at his mother—the woman who had raised him—with love and respect.

"I got to the car, got in, started it and Lydia suddenly went crazy. Said someone was after her. Before I could get the car turned off, she'd gotten out. She fell in the snow. I got her up. She hit me. I'd never been hit before. I've gotta tell you, I almost hit her back, but I didn't." Lydia looked at Billy. "I didn't."

"I believe you."

"But I pushed her. I wanted her away from me. She hit a piece of ice, and then, she hit the ground. I never saw anything like it. She just went down. Didn't try to catch herself or anything. She was pale, so pale. I could see blood from the back of her head, it was seeping onto the snow. And I just stood there. Just stood there."

"Maybe," Miles suggested, "we don't need to know every detail right now."

"I'm all right," Billy said.

Tamara had thought Miles was thinking of Lydia, but now, now that Billy answered, she suddenly saw what Lydia was seeing…still that two-year-old boy who needed protecting.

It was exactly what Lorraine Griffin would be seeing.

"There wasn't anything you could have done," Tamara said. "You weren't a nurse. You were a twenty-something girl."

"I could have lifted her head. I could have run inside the church and called someone. I—I must have stood there for ten minutes."

"You must have been in shock," Tamara said.

"Then what did you do?" Jake asked.

"I left her there in the snow. I don't know if she was dead or alive. And I'm ashamed because I felt dead inside. I went inside the church and called the bar. I knew Jasper was heading back there. Sure enough, he'd just gotten there. He got on the phone, and he came back to the church. It took him all of five minutes. Her lying there in the cold all that time."

"And?"

"She'd stopped bleeding. I was fool enough to think that was good, but it really meant she no longer needed to bleed. Jasper felt her neck and said she was dead."

The only sound in the room was breathing. It was loud. Finally, down the hall someone coughed.

"And you and the sheriff put her in the fallout shelter," Tamara finished for Lydia.

"Jasper about fainted. He'd just come from the bar and was already upset. Not sure what all happened there, but it had something to do with the Livingston dad. Jasper was muttering about not letting another child get hurt. At first, I didn't understand, but when his mutterings finally made sense, I knew he was right."

Tamara knew they were getting a condensed version of the crime. But the pieces were falling into place. After seeing little Natalie, Lisa's baby, Tamara knew that she'd do anything to protect that innocent child.

Lorraine had done the same.

"It was snowing," Lydia continued, "so every mark we made while moving the body was soon covered. Only my family knew about the fallout shelter."

"Was it Grandpa's idea?" Jake asked.

"No, it was mine. The ground was frozen, so it's not like we could bury her. I meant to go back, later, do something. Maybe I thought that in the morning, it would all go away, and Lydia would traipse into the house, pick up Billy and life would go on." Lydia shook her head. "Everything was happening so fast. My cheek was still stinging from where she'd hit me. My arms hurt from trying to hold her up as I struggled to get her to the car. And I knew Jasper was right about what would happen to Billy. I knew that with her dead, and me probably in jail, and my parents so old, I knew Billy didn't have a chance. He'd be hurting, all his life, inside and out, and wind up like…"

"Like all the Frencis," Vince finished.

"You wouldn't have gone to jail," Tamara said. "A good lawyer would have—"

"I know that now, but I wasn't really thinking that night, and in the end, neither was Jake's grandfather. We were both thinking about Billy, about what was best for Billy. You said I was in shock. Well, believe me, both the sheriff and I were in shock. I look back at that night now, at all the mistakes we made, choices we made, and wonder that we kept our sanity." She reached out her hand for Billy. He took it, eyes misty, and held it to his cheek.

"I was wrong, so wrong," Lydia said.

Miles started to open his mouth, but Vince interrupted. "You were not wrong to do whatever was in your power to keep Billy away from Uncle Drew."

"Believe me," Miles added. "God knows about sacrifice."

"Wait!" Tamara protested. "I'm lost here. You're feeling horribly guilty because you had a wild sister who attacked you and then probably overdosed at your feet?"

"And I just stood there."

"Ma'am, you didn't stand still," Tamara said. "You knew your sister's history, and in the blink of an eye, you gave up your future. You became a mother overnight to make sure Billy had a chance."

"My grandfather never made a rash decision," Jake said. "If he helped you hide Lydia's body in the fallout shelter, then he had a reason, and I remember how personally he took it when it came to anytime a child got hurt."

"Mom," Billy said, "you didn't ask for her to show up at the church's door. You didn't deny her entry. You didn't ask for her to hit you. You didn't hit her back."

"But I was the mature one. The one who took care of her."

"She was of legal age and had a child," Tamara stated. "It was time for her to take charge of herself."

"Why was she so different from you?" Billy asked. "Why?"

"Why does any young person switch from everyday normal to everyday ugly?" Jake said. "Drugs."

"In Lydia's case, that was probably it. She got started in the wrong crowd right when we got into high school."

"But you didn't get into the wrong crowd, didn't use drugs. Why couldn't she have done the same?" Billy asked.

Tamara answered, "Lorraine was the strong one."

"And now you have to be strong," Lydia said to Billy. "Because the whole town's going to know, and if I go to jail, you have to make sure your family doesn't suffer."

"You won't go to jail," Jake said.

"You can't promise that," Lydia retorted.

Tamara piped up. "I'll represent you. I'll be getting my Nebraska license soon. I'll do your case, pro bono."

"It doesn't have to be pro bono," Billy said. "We have plenty of money. Mom practically owns all of Main Street. We can pay."

"I don't want the money." Tamara moved next to Lydia. "I've been reading all the old church bulletins, all the things you did at so young an age. You made me want to be a better person. You still do. You make me want to know the Lord who guided you."

"I'll tell you," Lydia promised.

As if knowing that a somber mood needed to be broken, Vince's cell phone rang.

"Sorry." Vince fumbled for his belt and grabbed his cell and stepped from the room. Tamara followed.

"It almost feels like the day-to-day world cannot still exist," Vince said after he hung up. "That was my boss. Tali's wanting to know why I've been gone for two hours on a mere lunch break."

"I've never heard anything remotely like what we just heard in there," Tamara whispered. "Imagine what that poor woman's gone through all these years, knowing that she might have caused her sister's death and yet raising her sister's son."

Vince said bitterly, "More of Uncle Drew's doing. There's still something wrong with this whole thing. Drew said he was keeping Lydia safe. When he said no one had spoken to Lydia in months, he wasn't thinking the Lydia we know. He was thinking about the real Lydia—the dead Lydia. That means he knew she was down in that room, too. How did he know?"

Tamara glanced in Lydia's room. It had again grown silent, but she could see Miles talking. Stepping in, she saw that he led a prayer. Billy clutched his mother's hand. Even Jake's face had a more relaxed look. Tamara heard the word *forgiveness*. She heard mention of a good name being more desirable than riches.

She turned to motion Vince into the room. He needed to hear this.

He was gone.

And he stayed gone.

After saying goodbye to Lydia and the others, Tamara headed for Yano's. Vince wasn't there; two days later, someone else had taken over the job. All Tamara could do was leave messages, never returned, on his cell phone. Tali only shook his head. "Not like Vince," he said.

Tamara, however, knew all about running.

Vince had never really read the Sherman newspaper. He preferred to get his news either by television or on the Internet. However, with Lydia Griffin as its lead story, the *Sherman Gazette* suddenly took on a new life.

It only took two days for the story to break. The reporter did a good job investigating. Two new items came to light. One, the reason why the bar experienced so many problems that long ago night had to do with a tainted batch of LSD. Two people were hospitalized. According to medical records, the batch of LSD was laced with strychnine, among other things.

No wonder Lydia thought she was being chased.

The other newsworthy item had to do with Drew Frenci, and not that he was Billy's birth father. It seemed Drew had been arrested for selling a small quantity of LSD a month before Lydia's death, only not in Sherman.

Vince wasn't surprised.

Drew was no help. For the first time that Vince could remember, he actually wanted to talk to his uncle, wanted to force Drew to talk about the past.

But Drew was now in intensive care, with double pneumonia. He'd soon, if the doctors were right, be out of their lives.

Vince Frenci's life was definitely on a sharp U-turn. For a while, with Tamara, he'd felt like a somebody. Not only that, he'd started feeling something for somebody. The wrong somebody.

Frencis hurt the people they loved. Look at Drew's life, look at Vince's father.

Vince wasn't about to hurt Tamara.

John Konrad hadn't been that excited about moving Vince, who he called his most capable employee, from an immediate job to a less immediate job, but Tali and Sharon were understandably agreeable when Vince was reassigned to repairing their daughter's basement's drywall.

She lived with her husband and kids on the outskirts of town. There was no Gloria Baker to hurry Vince along, no Tali or Sharon to ask questions and joke with. Tali's daughter did the busy work of a farm wife; the kids were in school.

Vince had never felt so alone. Maybe because until Tamara he'd never *wanted* to be with someone 24/7. She'd gotten under his skin and headed right to his heart. Their pairing spelled disaster, though, and because he loved her—yes, loved her—he'd do the right thing. Distance himself. Even ask to be transferred from working on Tali's restaurant.

It was harder than he'd imagined because it meant distancing himself from everyone who mattered in his small world. When Tamara had been by his side, nothing had seemed small. It wasn't that she made the world seem big. It was that she made the world seem alive.

Funny how quickly Tamara made friends. Vince couldn't go see Lydia; Tamara was her most devoted visitor. Vince heard that talking about the Bible took up most of their time. Next thing Vince heard Tamara had accepted Jesus and had been baptized. Vince couldn't eat at Yano's, where because Vince was helping Tali and

Sharon's daughter, a free lunch came as a benefit, because Tamara was right across the street. Vince couldn't even stop by and bellyache to Alex. Not only was his best friend too busy with baby Natalie, but Alex was Tamara's brother-in-law.

Truth was, Vince missed Tamara.

Before Tamara, getting off work, then sitting in front of the television seemed a good life.

Now the only person Vince seemed able to talk to was Miles. Preachers were good listeners but they tended to talk a lot, too. From Miles, Vince learned all he was missing—namely fellowship.

Lydia's, make that Lorraine's, parents had known about the body in the fallout shelter. When Lorraine had got home that night, she'd fallen apart. Her father had gotten the story of Lydia out of her.

It had been his idea to send Lorraine away. At first, Lorraine thought it was to protect Billy, but later, she'd realized it was because of her father's position, his reputation. He didn't want a family scandal.

Lorraine, already fragile, hadn't been up to fighting him about anything.

Vince couldn't fathom how Lorraine had lived with her secrets all these years.

Miles simply said something about faith.

Miles also said he had both Tommy and Jimmy working at the church as part of their community service. Good. Vince intended to inspire a little community service of his own from Jimmy. Drew's yard still was in disrepair. The money Jimmy had taken from Drew wasn't enough to cover the damages to Tamara's building, so Jimmy was going to work to pay off the rest. The car he wanted was an oh-so-distant dream.

Needless to say, Jimmy wasn't talking to Vince.

Outside of work, only Miles was talking to Vince.

As Vince flipped from one station to another, it seemed an empty way of life.

Empty way of life?

Where had he heard that term before? Oh, yeah, from the preacher.

Who got it from the Bible.

Vince went and got the Bible the preacher had given him—the result of starting a friendship with a preacher—and started flipping through it, and finally settled on simply reading what the preacher had written in the margins of the New Testament.

After an hour, the tiniest nudge inspired Vince to pull his cell phone from his belt. Once he made the call, there was no turning back. If he knew Miles Pynchon, the preacher would drop everything and come, not to retrieve the Bible, but to preach the Word.

Instead, the phone rang, and the caller ID read Miles Pynchon.

"Preacher," Vince greeted him. "I was about to call you."

"Good," Miles said. "I'd love to talk. I spoke a lot to Tamara yesterday. She came to church."

Funny, the words came from the preacher, but they weren't as upbeat as usual.

"Something wrong with Tamara?" Vince asked.

"No, oh, no. But I'm here with your uncle. He's asking for you."

"What does he want me for?"

"It's got to be about Lydia."

"How'd you get involved?"

"I come to the hospital every Monday evening.

There are usually two or three people I know who could use a visit. Gloria tried to get ahold of your mother, but that wasn't what Drew wanted. He wants you. Gloria came and got me because Drew was getting agitated, and because she knows he's dying, and she knows there's something he wants to get off his chest."

"Has he said anything?"

"No, but I'm not who he wants to talk to. He's asking for Tamara, too. Gloria tried to reach her, but Tamara's not answering her cell phone."

"That's odd. Tamara always answers."

"Not today."

Looked like this Monday night was about to get interesting. "I'm on my way," Vince said, after getting Drew's new room number.

There were a few cars on the road. The convenience store did a booming business. Yano's was still open for business; the parking lot was half-full. On Tamara's side of the street, the bookstore was dark, as was the antique store. The light in the Amhurst Church's attic glowed.

Vince remembered that Miles said she wasn't answering her cell phone. Maybe he should call.

No.

She was rebuilding her life, setting up her law practice and preparing to defend Lydia Griffin.

And his uncle's shadow was over the whole case, as an errant father, as a drug dealer and who knows what else.

Visiting hours were over, but no one stopped Vince as he made his way through the hospital lobby. Drew was now on the fifth floor. Vince had to call the nurses' station to be buzzed in. The minute he gave his name, the door opened.

Miles sat in the visitor's chair, a Bible in his hand. "I guess he's been loaded for bear for the past few hours. Gloria thinks someone turned the television on, and whatever Drew heard set him off."

"She's right," Drew growled. It didn't sound threatening as it was followed by a wheeze. "Gloria Baker always knew more than was good. Boy, come here."

Vince knew he was Boy.

"The news said that Lorraine Griffin's going to be charged with murder."

"That's right," Vince said. "Ly—Lorraine's more or less confessed."

"Jasper Ramsey still alive?"

"He's not physically or mentally able to answer any questions," Miles supplied.

"Then, it's just Lorraine."

Vince wasn't sure if Drew was asking a question or making a statement.

"I saw it on the news." Drew stared at the dark television. "It showed a picture of her. She's gotten old, but she still looks good." He coughed. "Her twin probably would still look good. She was a pretty little gal. I didn't do right by her."

A few weeks ago, Vince might have added, *You haven't done right by anyone.*

"Drew," Vince said. "Why did you say you needed to keep Lydia safe? I thought you were talking about the Lydia we all know, but you weren't, you were talking about the real Lydia. How did you know she was down there?"

"I saw them dragging her down there."

"Why didn't you tell someone?"

Drew stopped looking at the television. "They

showed Billy and his family. I didn't think he looked much like me, at first, but then they showed some pictures from his childhood, and they showed his girls, women now. I could see it, then, a bit." This time the cough was more choked, lasted longer, and left Drew out of breath. The sound of the clock ticking suddenly seemed loud. Finally, Drew got a second wind. "But in them pictures all them kids were smiling. Smiling because they had a good life. Thanks to Lorraine, they had a good life."

"That doesn't answer why you didn't tell anyone about Lydia's body." Vince pointed out.

"I didn't tell anyone," Drew wheezed, "because leaving her down there meant I'd never have to pay child support. Leaving her down there meant no one would ask questions about how much LSD she'd taken and why only three people got so sick. Three people I was mad at."

"You were mad at Lydia?" Vince asked.

"Sure I was. She wanted more help with Billy. She wanted money for child support, and yet she wanted me to stop taking things from the church. And she told me she wanted to stop doing drugs. The only time she was fun was when she was on drugs."

Vince didn't know how to respond. Throughout all the years he'd known Drew, he'd known his uncle was an awful man.

Awful didn't begin to describe Drew.

"I'm not mad anymore," Drew said.

No, he was old and sad and dying.

"I can see in your eyes what you think of me, boy. I could always see."

Vince didn't respond.

"And you were right."

A nurse opened the door, came in and started taking Drew's blood pressure. Miles stood up. "I need to leave."

"No," Drew said. "I want someone besides Vince to hear this. I know all about having witnesses and such. Since the nurse is here, now's a good time."

The nurse looked ready to run. Her foot did a tap-tap-tap, even as she pumped on the arm band.

"Lorraine didn't kill Lydia."

The nurse's foot stopped tapping. Miles sat down.

"That night, I followed Lydia to the old church. I just wanted to make sure she didn't say anything or do anything to get me in trouble. That bartender didn't need to call the police. I could have gotten her under control. Things were going from bad to worse." His voice gained strength, as if unburdening his heart was unburdening his chest. "Sure surprised me when Lorraine got spunky. I knew the minute Lorraine thought her sister was dead. Wasn't but a second later, I saw Lydia raise her head just a smidgen. She wasn't dead. But when Lorraine went in and called Jasper, I made sure her worst nightmare came true. At the time, killing her seemed like the solution to a lotta problems. I simply walked over and covered her face."

"We need Jake," Miles said.

Drew's face slackened. His eyes closed. "Tell the coroner. I suffocated Lydia. It didn't take long. But once Jasper got there and Lorraine babbled her story, he only bent down and checked her pulse. He was crying too hard to do anything else. I never saw anything like it. Big ol' sheriff crying like a baby."

"What was Lorraine doing?" Vince asked.

"Standing there looking like she was ready to fall

down. I think watching her sway is when I realized what I'd done."

"You think?" Vince asked snidely.

"I'd fathered a child with her and yet I didn't feel any real grief at her death. There was payback, though. Last time anyone really loved me was Lydia, and that was almost fifty years ago." As if his strength was gone and there was nothing left, Drew closed his eyes.

"God loved you then, and He loves you now," Miles said gently.

Drew opened his eyes and looked at Vince. "Don't be like me," he whispered. "Don't be like me."

Without Vince, working on the old church was no fun. On Monday evening, Tamara painted until her body ached and her eyes could barely stay open. Hunter-green was the perfect color for her office. Next week, she'd go ahead and move in some chairs, a filing cabinet, a few decent lamps.

Outside, a full moon guided her home.

She still drove her sister's car. Maybe an economy car would be a smart choice. She didn't miss the Jag; she actually liked the extra legroom.

The lights were on in the main house. Billy was as busy as Tamara, working on making changes and getting ready not only for his wife to arrive but to also bring his mother home. The front porch had the tools of the trade displayed: an empty paint can, a tarp, etc. There was a basement apartment he was modifying. Lydia would have her own space but be with Billy and his family for the rest of her life.

Tamara parked in the street and hurried up the sidewalk. She had the upstairs apartment for as long as she needed, Billy said.

He'd also lowered the rent on the downtown properties and was pitching in to help repair the damages done by the tornado.

She hurried up the stairs and unlocked the door to her apartment.

Her hand stilled as moonlight caught the reflection on her watch. It was midnight. William Massey's favorite hour. Her steps faltered even as the door opened.

She heard the music too late.

SIXTEEN

It was midnight when Vince returned to his truck. The sheriff had been called, but Drew had fallen asleep before Jake could question him. Vince settled behind the wheel. For some reason, he was half-tempted to call Tamara. She'd be interested in knowing everything Drew said.

Don't be like me.

Alone. Drew had pushed people away his entire life. Vince wasn't like that. He had friends, good friends, like Alex and now Miles. And Vince certainly didn't push family away. He'd always been there to help his mother and take care of Jimmy.

Of course, he'd done a good job of staying single, but that had never bothered him until now.

There were other things, too, he needed to tell Tamara. Things that had nothing to do with Drew or the old church or Lydia. Things that had everything to do with never being alone again and with having hope.

The lights were off at Tamara's church building. He wondered what she'd done to the inside for the past three days. She'd carried enough paint in to coat the whole building. She'd often exited wearing enough paint to make him smile.

Don't be like me.

Not a chance, Vince thought.

Don't be like me... That had been Miles's lesson that one Wednesday. Drew was like that man Lazarus. Only tonight Vince heard Drew's warning. On a whim, he turned down Tamara's street. The lights were on in Lydia's portion of the house. Maybe Billy was awake and working. Jake had called Billy, so Billy knew about Drew's confession.

Had Billy told Tamara?

Jake, like Miles, couldn't reach Tamara.

She wasn't answering her phone.

Parking in the street, behind Tamara's borrowed car, Vince went to the front door and tapped softly. If Billy was asleep, then Vince didn't want to wake him.

No one answered.

But the door was ajar.

Feeling a bit guilty, Vince pushed it all the way open. Billy lay on the living-room floor.

"Billy?"

A moan was the response.

Vince hurried in, dropped to his knees and felt for a pulse. It was there, strong, but Billy wasn't moving. Vince grabbed for his cell phone, dialed 911 and then stopped.

An operator said, "Nine-one-one, what is your emergency?"

Vince opened his mouth to answer, only to shut it as a sound came from upstairs. Someone was moving upstairs. Could Tamara be up there unaware of what was happening down here? The sound of music, a song Vince didn't know, played in the silence. Tamara played country music. It was the one thing that didn't seem to fit her personality. Everything else about her was classical.

Vince caught a few of the song's lyrics just as Tamara screamed.

"The Midnight Hour."

Vince jumped up, shouted the address into the phone and ran to the front door.

He climbed the stairs to her apartment, two at a time, praying all the way, and when he discovered the door was locked, opened it with one well-placed kick.

William Massey, who Vince recognized from newspaper articles he'd read about Tamara's stalker, stood before him, shifting from one foot to the other.

"Who is this? Why is he coming over during our time?" Massey had Tamara around the neck with a hand—the one hand that remained steady. With his other hand, the shaky one, he withdrew a knife from his belt.

Vince wasn't afraid of a knife, but he was afraid of what a knife would do to Tamara before he could cross the room.

"You don't want to hurt her. She likes your music. She told me all about this song," Vince said.

The music continued playing.

Vince looked around the room, careful not to move too much and startle Massey. "I'm surprised they didn't notify Tamara about your release," Vince said conversationally.

Tamara hiccuped. Massey looked at her, and Vince took a tiny step toward them, saying, "I mean, they're supposed to, right?"

"I dropped my phone in the paint," Tamara whispered. She was so still only her mouth moved. "I've been so busy working on the church, I didn't even try to clean it yet."

Tamara's eyes finally left the knife and went to Vince.

She didn't look nearly as scared as she had when he first burst in. Her look was full of trust and hope.

"How did you manage to get released?" Vince asked. "Or did you escape?"

"Finally," Massey said, "the law worked like it was supposed to. Tamara never should have testified against me. Some of her testimony was a bit too parallel to the previous case, almost verbatim. My new lawyer finally got the judge to admit Tamara inadvertently used some information that should have been confidential, sacred, between lawyer and client."

Down the street came the first wail of the police siren.

"I wish I'd been the judge," Vince snarled. "You'd never see the light of day."

"How did you find me?" Tamara whispered.

"I did an Internet search for your name. One of the first things I found was the purchase of that old church. Then, too, your name's been in the Sherman paper more than once because of vandalism and again when you found that dead body."

It took every ounce of Vince's willpower not to rush Massey.

"What did you hit Billy with?" Vince asked.

Massey smiled. "I didn't hit Billy. Who's Billy?"

"The man downstairs."

"Actually," came a weak voice from the doorway, "you did hit me, but maybe not hard enough." Billy Griffin held a gun.

"I didn't figure you for one who would own a gun," Vince said.

"The restaurant I managed was robbed two times in one month. My wife got this for me the following Christmas."

"Remind me to thank her," Vince said, as he yanked

the gun from Billy's fingers, surprising Billy and completely taking Massey off guard. "Drop," Vince ordered Tamara.

She did.

As she dropped, she managed to kick Massey behind the knees. His feet came out from under him and he toppled.

In a moment, Vince was on top of him, gun pointed to the back of his neck, and the order of "Don't move" spewing from his lips.

Tamara slid Massey's knife under the rug.

Outside the siren choked to a stop. After a moment, policemen clambered up the stairs. One of the cops took the gun from Vince's hand. Another helped Tamara to her feet. Billy let another cop lead him to the kitchen table and then to a chair.

"He took the key to your place, Tamara," Billy said. "Mom had it labeled on a pegboard right by the back door. It probably didn't take him but a minute to find it after he clobbered me."

"What made you stop by?" Tamara asked Vince.

Vince took her in his arms. He didn't care who saw or what they said about it later. The kiss was immediate and urgent, and proved that they'd both made it.

Together.

"It was Uncle Drew's suggestion," Vince said when Tamara finally drew away. "He said, *Don't be like me. I figured the best way to make sure I didn't wind up like him was to start right away and be honest with you.*"

"At midnight?"

"You weren't answering your phone. That scared me. Plus, I knew you had trouble sleeping. I figured if you were awake, I'd tell you that you didn't need to worry about Lydia. She didn't kill her sister. Plus, I didn't want to let another minute go by without telling you I..."

He paused, the words sticking in his throat. He couldn't remember the last time he'd said to anyone *I love you.*

Vince stepped over a sled and knocked on Alex and Lisa's door. His heart no longer hurt. Since the beginning of December, it had been one family get-together right after another. Some had been good.

Lydia Griffin went home the first week of December. Billy and his wife were all settled into the main part of the house; they'd already placed membership at the Main Street Church. Billy had gone to work at Yano's. Not too many people in town knew that the new day manager not only got a weekly paycheck from Tali but also deserved the title of landlord. Nearly the whole town showed up for Lydia's homecoming.

Other get-togethers had not been so good.

Drew Frenci died the second week of December. Unfortunately, he never regained consciousness, and never got to answer the questions so many wanted to ask. He'd been buried on a cold Thursday morning when snow covered the ground and the skies were a gloomy dark gray. Miles said a few words, very generic. Vince listened to every word. They were from the Bible, the Bible he'd been reading every night. The one that contained words about hope.

Be joyful in hope, patient in affliction, faithful in prayer.

Because of Miles Pynchon and the Main Street Church, the burial didn't consist of just Frencis. Quite a few people attended, all from the church. Gloria was one of them. She sat in the second row, right behind

Vince's little brother Jimmy. When the service ended, she hugged every one of the Frencis, but she stayed in front of Jimmy the longest.

Finally, when Jimmy began to shift uncomfortably from one foot to the other, she smiled. "I have something for you."

She handed him something wrapped in brown paper.

For the past few months, under Vince's supervision, Jimmy had been busy with repairs for both Tamara and Gloria, all in the name of reparations.

It looked like he'd repaired a lot more than physical damage.

With the speed only a teenage boy could manage, the brown paper hit the ground. What was left in Jimmy's grasp was the old Bible.

"He can't accept that," Vince said quickly.

"Nonsense," Gloria said. "This Bible is worth thousands of dollars." She looked at Jimmy. "You can sell it and buy that car you've been dreaming of, or you can keep it and read it."

Jimmy looked from his mother to Vince to Gloria. "Do I have to decide now?"

The words told Vince that during the past few months, God had been working in his little brother's life, too.

Last week, Vince had been introduced to a different kind of family when he and Tamara attended the church's Christmas party together. Vince's mother and little brother attended, too. Afterward, Vince had asked Miles to baptize him. Miles didn't need to be asked twice.

Tonight, on Christmas Eve, Vince was Tamara's date for her family's gathering.

Date? Nah, not a strong enough word. Vince patted his jacket pocket for the hundredth time. Date? Not a strong enough word for a man who hoped, prayed, to become a permanent fixture in Tamara's life. He'd knocked on Alex's door many a time. As a friend. Tonight, he felt like so much more. If all went as planned, someday their children could play together.

The door finally opened and there stood Tamara. Her glorious red hair wasn't perfectly styled; instead it was pulled back into a ponytail because already little Natalie, at only a few months old, knew how to pull. Tamara had also learned to relax a little. Flannel shirts never looked so good as when she wore them.

Neither did jeans.

He felt Tamara's fingers coming around his upper arm, and she tugged him toward her, in out of the cold.

"About time you got here."

The smell of turkey roasting combined with some sort of cinnamon apple scent. Tamara's mom and sister were putting together a puzzle with Amy, Lisa and Alex's oldest daughter.

Vince stopped. His mother and little brother were here, too.

"Mom?"

Before she could answer, Tamara said, "I ran into them at the store this morning. Lisa makes way too much food so we needed more people."

"It's not Lisa making too much food," Alex argued. He wore an apron and carried a spatula. A hand towel was draped over one shoulder. As if proof was needed, Lisa came from the hallway carrying little Natalie.

They all welcomed Vince in out of the cold. None of them stopped what they were doing. He was already a part of their lives.

He felt it.

He loved it.

"I just finished setting the table," Tamara said.

"Pitch in with the puzzle," Sheila, Tamara's middle sister, suggested. "We're stuck."

"Only ten minutes until supper's ready," Alex advised. "Vince, you cut it close to the wire."

"I had something to do."

He'd gone straight from work to the jewelers. The ring was perfect and, he hoped, the right size. Maybe Tamara would go for a drive with him after dinner? Of course, maybe he should talk to her mother, first. He'd met Mrs. Jacoby two days ago when he and Tamara drove to Omaha to pick her family up.

The mother was quiet, but Sheila asked enough questions to fill a book.

Then again, maybe Vince should hold off until a romantic night. He'd take her to dinner—not Yano's. Everyone would laugh if Vince got down on his knees.

Vince would laugh, too.

He patted his pocket again. Still there.

"Oh, look," Tamara exclaimed.

The television was on, turned down low, and until now no one had been looking at it. No one except Tamara.

"Remember," she told Vince. "I told you about *It's a Wonderful Life*. You said you'd never seen it."

"Never seen it!" Lisa exclaimed. "It's a classic."

Tamara's hand still curved around Vince's arm. She tugged him over to the couch.

"Let him take his coat off," Alex advised before heading back to the kitchen.

Carefully, Vince took off his jacket, tucking it next to him and settling down next to Tamara. It was hard to pay attention to the television when he wanted to pay attention to her.

"You've turned our big sister into such a girl," Sheila accused, shaking a puzzle piece at him.

"Oh, I was always a girl," Tamara said, laughing. "I just needed the right boy." She finally took her eyes off the television.

Vince, however, was looking at the show's opening: the music and the title dominating the screen.

It's a Wonderful Life.

He grabbed his jacket and pulled the tiny box from a pocket. He flipped it open, turned to Tamara, and said, "I tried to say 'I love you' once before, but the words wouldn't come. I guess God was letting me know I had a few things to sort out, but I don't want to waste any more time figuring things out by myself. Not when I can have you by my side. Marry me, Tamara."

Her mouth opened, then closed.

"What?" he asked. "Do you need counsel before answering? Want to consult the jury?"

The lawyer didn't have a comeback, a rebuttal, a closing argument.

A verdict.

Instead, she leaned over, took his hand, and said, "So, together, you want to make a wonderful life?"

Never mind the audience. He cupped her chin and pulled her toward him, almost onto his lap.

"If I say yes," Tamara whispered, "it's a life sentence. No chance of parole."

"If you say yes?" Vince questioned.

"*When* I say yes," she corrected. "Yes, yes, yes."

Before he started the kiss and sealed the beginning of forever, he whispered, "It's already a wonderful life. Since the first time I saw you."

* * * * *

Dear Reader,

The seed for *Clandestine Cover-Up* was planted a good five years ago as I sat in a church in the small town of Ash Fork, Arizona. My friend's husband is the minister there. Yes, the church started its life as a house. Oh, if only those walls could talk, offer opinions and—gasp—gossip. I did listen to the sermon (but it was five years ago so I've forgotten the topic), but I also thought about the church buildings and how we use them. It made me think about how, no matter where I attend, I sit on the right side, toward the back. Hmm. The tradition started with my parents in Omaha, Nebraska. I took it with me to college in Texas. And, in Arizona, today, I'm still honoring it. If I sit somewhere else, it feels funny. In Ash Fork, where there were only about seven rows of pews, my family was on pew six (seven was taken) on the right side. Where I sit is part of my history. I've been in many church buildings over the years. My hero and heroine, Tamara and Vince, have not. As I wrote the book, I realized that one of their journeys would be figuring out that a church building is so much more. It's the fabric of life, the fabric that comforts and builds memories. Thank you for reading *Clandestine Cover-Up*. I enjoy hearing from readers. You may contact me at www.pamelakayetracy.com or at Pamela Tracy, c/o Steeple Hill Books, 233 Broadway Suite 1001, New York, NY 10279. Or please visit my blog: http://ladiesofsuspense.blogspot.com.

Pamela Tracy

QUESTIONS FOR DISCUSSION

1. At the beginning of *Clandestine Cover-Up,* Tamara is standing still on the sidewalk. She can move forward or she can step back. She is completely at a crossroads. Because she doesn't want to "always" run scared, she decides to move forward. Have you ever faced a hard decision where you moved forward, yet didn't quite believe you should?

2. In many ways, Vince is a contradiction. He's single with few responsibilities, yet he is a valued and reliable worker. What, in his past, keeps him from believing in relationships? What in his past helped him to have a work ethic that in many ways shaped him into an honorable man? What contradictions have shaped your life?

3. In the old Amhurst Church, the attic seemed to call to Tamara. Part of the reason is she can see the heartbeat (a thriving downtown of personalities) of Sherman, Nebraska, when she looks out the attic window. If you could have a window to watch one spot of the world, what would your window be aimed at?

4. Vince has to deal with his uncle Drew quite often during the book. Do you have an Uncle Drew in your life? What are some hints in dealing with the hard-to-like, impossible-to-reach people we encounter in daily life?

5. Lisa, Tamara's sister, is a fairly new and very enthusiastic Christian. Think about someone you

know who is new to Christ and enthralled with the riches offered. What are they most excited about? Now think…are you just as excited about the same thing? Do you need (want) to be?

6. One of the issues Tamara deals with is how others treated her during and after the stalking. Her fiancé was of the "get over it" mentality. Can you think of a time when you faced a dilemma and the people around you didn't react quite as you needed them to? Have you ever wished you could change a reaction you offered to a friend during a time of need?

7. Gloria Baker is a preacher's daughter who knows the history of the Amhurst Church. Tamara is most impressed by the photos of Gloria's life and what they depict. Think about your favorite photos. What do they say about you?

8. In Gloria's house, there's a cross-stitch of a mansion that says, My Mansion Will Not Fade With Time. What exactly does that mean? What does your mansion look like?

9. During a tornado, Tamara and Vince take shelter in a fallout shelter. How interesting to find one in the basement of an old building. Think about the man who had it built. Why would he do such a thing? When you take shelter, where do you go? Think physically and figuratively.

10. Mistaken identity, stolen identity. Lorraine Griffin takes over her sister's life for the sake of a child. Did

she overreact? Do the right thing? If she hadn't, what do you think might have happened to Billy?

11. Near the end, Uncle Drew says, "Don't be like me." Think about how powerful a command that is. Think about how many people "need" to say those words and listen to their own advice. Let's think of it the other way. In your discussion, think of someone you personally know who could say, "Do be like me." Now, list three reasons why they can say this.

12. Vince asks Tamara to share a wonderful life with him. He's doing this while the movie *It's a Wonderful Life* is on the television. What does a wonderful life mean to you? Is there a movie or song that has made an impression on you?

Here is an exciting sneak preview of
TWIN TARGETS by Marta Perry,
the first book in the new
6-book Love Inspired Suspense series
PROTECTING THE WITNESSES
available beginning January 2010.

Deputy U.S. Marshal Micah McGraw forced down the sick feeling in his gut. A law enforcement professional couldn't get emotional about crime victims. He could imagine his police chief father saying the words. Or his FBI agent big brother. They wouldn't let emotion interfere with doing the job.

"Pity." The local police chief grunted.

Natural enough. The chief hadn't known Ruby Maxwell, aka Ruby Summers. He hadn't been the agent charged with relocating her to this supposedly safe environment in a small village in Montana. He didn't have to feel responsible for her death.

"This looks like a professional hit," Chief Burrows said.

"Yeah."

He knew only too well what was in the man's mind. What would a professional hit man be doing in the remote reaches of western Montana? Why would anyone want to kill this seemingly inoffensive waitress?

And most of all, what did the U.S. Marshals Service have to do with it?

All good questions. Unfortunately he couldn't answer

any of them. Secrecy was the crucial element that made the Federal Witness Protection Service so successful. Breach that, and everything that had been gained in the battle against organized crime would be lost.

His cell buzzed and he turned away to answer it. "McGraw."

"You wanted the address for the woman's next of kin?" asked one of his investigators.

"Right." Ruby had a twin sister, he knew. She'd have to be notified. Since she lived back east, at least he wouldn't be the one to do that.

"Jade Summers. Librarian. Current address is 45 Rock Lane, White Rock, Montana."

For an instant Micah froze. "Are you sure of that?"

"'Course I'm sure."

After he hung up, Micah turned to stare once more at the empty shell that had been Ruby Summers. She'd made mistakes in her life, plenty of them, but she'd done the right thing in the end when she'd testified against the mob. She hadn't deserved to end up lifeless on a cold concrete floor.

As for her sister…

What exactly was an easterner like Jade Summers doing in a small town in Montana? If there was an innocent reason, he couldn't think of it.

Ruby must have tipped her off to her location. That was the only explanation, and the deed violated one of the major principles of witness protection.

Ruby had known the rules. Immediate family could be relocated with her. If they chose not to, no contact was permitted—ever.

Ruby's twin had moved to Montana. White Rock

was probably forty miles or so east of Billings. Not exactly around the corner from her sister.

But the fact that she was in Montana had to mean that they'd been in contact. And that contact just might have led to Ruby's death.

He glanced at his watch. Once his team arrived, he'd get back on the road toward Billings and beyond, to White Rock. To find Jade Summers and get some answers.

*Will Micah get to Jade in time to save
her from a similar fate?
Find out in TWIN TARGETS,
available January 2010
from Love Inspired Suspense.*

REQUEST YOUR FREE BOOKS!

2 FREE RIVETING INSPIRATIONAL NOVELS
PLUS 2 FREE MYSTERY GIFTS

Love Inspired
SUSPENSE

YES! Please send me 2 FREE Love Inspired® Suspense novels and my 2 FREE mystery gifts (gifts are worth about $10). After receiving them, if I don't wish to receive any more books, I can return the shipping statement marked "cancel". If I don't cancel, I will receive 4 brand-new novels every month and be billed just $4.24 per book in the U.S. or $4.74 per book in Canada. That's a savings of over 20% off the cover price. It's quite a bargain! Shipping and handling is just 50¢ per book.* I understand that accepting the 2 free books and gifts places me under no obligation to buy anything. I can always return a shipment and cancel at any time. Even if I never buy another book, the two free books and gifts are mine to keep forever.

123 IDN EYM2 323 IDN EYNE

Name	(PLEASE PRINT)	
Address		Apt. #
City	State/Prov.	Zip/Postal Code

Signature (if under 18, a parent or guardian must sign)

Mail to Steeple Hill Reader Service:
IN U.S.A.: P.O. Box 1867, Buffalo, NY 14240-1867
IN CANADA: P.O. Box 609, Fort Erie, Ontario L2A 5X3
Not valid to current subscribers of Love Inspired Suspense books.

Want to try two free books from another series?
Call 1-800-873-8635 or visit www.morefreebooks.com

LISUS09

Cheyenne Rhodes has
come to Redemption,
Oklahoma, to start anew,
not to make new friends.
But single dad
Trace Bowman isn't
about to let her hide her
heart away. He just needs
to convince Cheyenne that
Redemption is more than
a place to hide—it's also a
way to be found....

Look for

Finding Her Way Home

by

Linda Goodnight

*Available January
wherever books are sold.*

www.SteepleHill.com

Steeple
Hill®

LI87571

TITLES AVAILABLE NEXT MONTH
Available December 29, 2009

FINDING HER WAY HOME by Linda Goodnight
Redemption River

She came to Oklahoma to escape her past, but single dad Trace Bowman isn't about to let Cheyenne Rhodes hide her heart away. But will he stand by her when he learns the secret she's running from?

THE DOCTOR'S PERFECT MATCH by Irene Hannon
Lighthouse Lane

Dr. Christopher Morgan is *not* looking for love. Especially with Marci Clay. The physician and the waitress come from two very different worlds. Worlds that are about to collide in faith and love.

HER FOREVER COWBOY by Debra Clopton
Men of Mule Hollow

Mule Hollow, Texas, is chock-full of handsome cowboys. Veterinarian Susan Worth moves in, dreaming of meeting Mr. Right, who most certainly is *not* the gorgeous rescue worker blazing through town...or *is* he?

THE FAMILY NEXT DOOR by Barbara McMahon

Widower Joe Kincaid doesn't want his daughter liking their pretty new neighbor. His little girl's lost too much already. And he doesn't think the city girl will last a month in their small Maine town. But Gillian Parker isn't what he expected.

A SOLDIER'S DEVOTION by Cheryl Wyatt
Wings of Refuge

Pararescue jumper Vince Reardon doesn't want to accept Valentina Russo's heartfelt apologies for wrecking his motorcycle.... Until she shows this soldier what true devotion is really about.

MENDING FENCES by Jenna Mindel

Called home to care for her ailing mother, Laura Toivo finds herself in uncertain territory. With the help of neighbor Jack Stahl, she'll learn that life is all about connections, and that love is the greatest gift.

LICNMBPA1209